THE WONDERFUL
WORLD OF DOGS

THE WONDERFUL
WORLD OF DOGS

Compiled by BETH BROWN

Pictures by LEONARD SHORTALL

HARPER & BROTHERS

Publishers   NEW YORK

THE WONDERFUL WORLD OF DOGS

Grateful acknowledgment is made to the following for permission to reprint selections included in this book:

"Blinkie" by Beth Brown; copyright © 1956 by Beth Brown; by permission of Prentice Hall, Inc.

"The Lost Dog Brings A Gift" by Anne Elizabeth Wilson; by permission of Andrew MacLean Limited.

"Choirboy" by Paul Annixter; copyright © 1957 by Paul Annixter; by permission of the author.

"Hurry Home, Candy" by Meindert DeJong; copyright 1953 by Meindert DeJong; by permission of Harper & Brothers.

"A Dog Like Pierre" by Ethel McCall Head; copyright © 1958 by Boy Scouts of America; by permission of the author and *Boys' Life* published by the Boy Scouts of America.

"The Sheep and the Dog;" *Aesop's Fables.*

"Jean Labadie's Big Black Dog" from *The Talking Cat* by Natalie Savage Carlson; copyright 1952 by Natalie Savage Carlson; by permission of Harper and Brothers.

"Wee Joseph" by William MacKellar; copyright © 1957 by William MacKellar; by permission of Whittlesey House, a division of McGraw-Hill Book Company.

"The 7th Pup" by Doris Gates; copyright 1947 by Doris Gates; by permission of the author.

"The Christmas Hunt" by Borden Deal; copyright © 1960 by The Curtis Publishing Company.

"The Strange Dog" by Russell Gordon Carter from *Young Readers Dog Stories;* copyright 1951 by Russell Gordon Carter; by permission of Lantern Press, Inc.

"The Comet" from *Frank of Freedom Hill* by Samuel A. Derieux; copyright 1921 by Mary Derieux; by permission of Doubleday & Company.

"The Coward" from *The Critter and Other Dogs* by Albert Payson Terhune; copyright 1936 by Albert Payson Terhune; by permission of Harper & Brothers.

"Gun-shy" from *Us and the Duchess* by Edward Fenton; copyright 1945, 1946, 1947 by Edward Fenton; by permission of Doubleday & Company, Inc.

"Old Yeller" by Fred Gipson; copyright © 1956 by Fred Gipson; by permission of Harper & Brothers and Hodder & Stoughton Limited.

"Mine Enemy's Dog" from *Fraternity Village* by Ben Ames Williams; by permission of Houghton Mifflin Company.

For
Roland H. Guinzburg
who gave my dogs a bowl of sky

Contents

THE WONDERFUL
WORLD OF DOGS

Blinkie

by Beth Brown

HE ALWAYS KNEW when it was morning. A cool wind would come down from the sky and touch his eyes and wake him. And all the world of sound and smell would come alive all around him—the birds in the old apple orchard—the scent of wild grass in the meadow—the cacophony of newborn peepers in the pond.

Blinkie was always the first dog to wake up at Sunnyside. He loved to greet the wind of early morning as it broke through the dark horizon of night and came over the hill, up the driveway, and into his private pen.

But on this particular morning, he awoke earlier than usual. There was a reason for this. The leash Mr. Johnson had bought him dangled precariously from his peg in the bunkhouse. The letter Mr. Johnson had promised to write was already four months late. His life depended on that letter.

For the past four months, the arrival of the postman constituted the most important moment of his day.

1

Blinkie had come to know the sound of the postman's car. Its familiar chug and its panting wait as it attended at the altar of the mailbox had become a daily ritual in Blinkie's troubled life. He knew the exact time of its coming. He followed the last echo as it rumbled through the gate and was lost upon his world.

Blinkie's senses were remarkably acute even for a wire-haired Terrier. He had suffered a great loss and this was nature's coin of compensation. He could smell for miles beyond the usual canine ken. He could taste the very wind upon his tongue. He could catch the faintest sound in the far reaches of space—as far away as the entrance gate—and beyond that to the great open highway which led to a home of one's own where freedom was the companion.

The experience at Christmas time in the Johnson flat had changed Blinkie. He knew what it was to have his earth self transformed into a rarefied being. Sunnyside was now one vast mountain of sound to him with its heartbeat as loud as a drum.

There were many sounds here at Sunnyside. Each sound belonged to something or someone, as much a part of that being as the body in which it traveled across the air waves to Blinkie.

Limpy, the Sunnyside cook, made one kind of sound. His hobble was his music. Rollo, the groom, had a reedy whistle. That was his instrument. Jock, the chauffeur, made martial music as he roared up the driveway. There was Doc Allbright, the veterinarian, playing a caress on the violin of his voice. There was Julie, small yet powerful, as she pounded at the piano keys and leaned back to rest against the echoes. Each one was an instrument in the orchestra, with Parrish, the proprietor, hammering away at the brassy cymbals like a savage giant creating thunderbolts.

Blinkie's hearing reached out to take in everyone—everything—voices and footsteps and vehicles—the daily procession of cars which brought the butcher, the baker, and most important of all, the buyer into the realms of Sunnyside.

These days, however, the postman was his chief concern. He knew what would happen if that letter failed to reach Parrish. And today was the last of the month.

Blinkie tried to be brave. He tried to push his fears aside.

After all, here was a new day, bright and shining as a new coin, and, like a new coin, apt to come down face up in a change of luck for Blinkie. It was good to be up, to throw back the cold blanket of night and bathe his small body in the warm rays of the morning.

It was high time to wake up the others. He stood up, lifted his head, cleared his throat—and emitted a loud, piercing bark.

Then he waited. He did not have long to wait.

"Morning, Geisha!"

"Morning, Blinkie!"

"Morning, Dandy!"

"Morning, Blinkie!"

"Morning, Golden Boy!"

"Good morning!" sang Golden Boy blithely. The Cocker rolled out of his little white house and clawed the earth to get rid of the excess energy he had stored up during the night. "Hello, Blink! Hello, everybody!"

"Morning, Galaxy!"

Galaxy, the Boxer, streaked up his runway and skidded to a stop at the wire enclosure. "Hi, Blinkie!"

"How!" crowed Brandy, the carefree Irish Setter. "How-do-you-doodle-doo!"

Now the others took to playing and bathing in the sunlight flooding their quarters.

There was Gypsy, the Foxhound, who lived two doors down the lane—Her Majesty, the English Bulldog, who lived three doors away—Handsome, the Great Dane, who lived just behind Blinkie—and Happy, the lively little Terrier, who occupied the pen at the very end of the row.

One by one, Blinkie had come to know these comrades in captivity. From time to time, he made the casual acquaintance of the various guests at Sunnyside whom he met in the barbershop, at the Infirmary, or as they promenaded past his pen. These colleagues walked the same earth with him. They shared the same sky. But they did not share the secret realm of his mind, dark though it was. The only happiness he had ever known was here in the magic world of orchard.

Here in the orchard, each dog had his own neat little house, painted a dazzling white. Each house had its own front porch. Each pen had its own runway, its own front gate and even its own little garden. Some of the gardens were festooned by a tree. Blinkie was one of the lucky ones. An old apple tree grew beside his door. He loved the cool trunk and the broad branches which opened wide their motherly arms as if to gather him in.

Here, in his little garden, Blinkie would lie—listening, dreaming, and at times talking aloud as if the apple tree could hear what he said and could give counsel to his troubled thinking.

Today, its branches were thick with springtime bloom. The scent was so rich that even Brandy, whose mind seldom foraged beyond food, sniffed in audible appreciation.

"That tree of yours sure smells good."

"It's in full bloom."

"What's the matter, Pal?"

"Nothing."

"You seem blue."

"Yeah. What is it?" persisted Duchess. "What's eating you?"

"I'd rather not say."

"I know," came sagely from Geisha. "It's that letter—"

"Maybe it'll come today," consoled Galaxy.

"There's still tomorrow," reflected Golden Boy.

"Tomorrow?" echoed Blinkie dully. "Tomorrow will be too late." He stared into a void filled with darkness and despair.

"That man Johnson sure handed you a raw deal," declared Dandy. "But what else can you expect from mankind?"

"Look at me!" wailed Geisha. "I got a swift kick, too."

"And what's wrong with you?"

"You ought to know. I've told you often enough. It's been six months since the family's been to see me."

"You can put me down for eight," computed Galaxy.

"Eight months—eight days—eight hours. I don't know why they go on paying my board."

"Yeah. My folks think they're keeping me in clover just 'cause I'm registered at Sunnyside. I would do without the clover if they'd only take me home."

"What's the matter, boys and girls?" came cheerfully from Brandy. Brandy was always lighthearted even on rainy days. Nothing ever disturbed the Red Setter. "Don't you like these gilded lodgings and the tasty grub you get?"

"Oh, I like it all right—as places go—" admitted Galaxy grudgingly. "But if you ask me, dogs belong with people and people belong with dogs."

"And dogs belong at home," added Her Majesty.

"Home!" echoed Geisha. "I keep dreaming about the big red house with the green garden, front and back. I wonder if I'll ever see it again."

"I'll probably be right here till I die," wailed Gypsy. "Like a bear in a zoo or a monkey behind bars or a bird in a net." Gypsy sighed. "I was meant to run—to leap—to fly—to find adventure for my four legs."

"Why can't we have our own world?" demanded Trojan. "A world without them!" He dreamed aloud. "We could roam the woods and be free. We could swim the seas and be strong. We could hunt for our food—"

"Yeah. We wouldn't have to sit up pretty and beg for every bone we get—"

"Forever free!" breathed Challenger. "A new regime for dogdom!"

"It sounds wonderful!"

"Pipe dream!"

"All right! Let me dream!"

"You said it, Geisha!"

"When do we leave for the wide-open spaces?" demanded Dandy.

"The wide-open spaces—" murmured Handsome. "Escape!" The Great Dane lifted his nose to the sky. "One of these days I'm going to escape—"

"Yep! And they'll go after you and bring you right back. You'll get a sleeping pill for your trouble and Parrish will cross you off the register—"

"I lived in the woods once," reminisced Gypsy. "I was free as a bird on the wing—"

"You're not the only one, Gypsy. I policed a cattle range out on the plains of Texas."

"Tell us about it, Gala."

"Well, there were no fences to keep me out—nor doors to lock me in. It was just wide-open horizon as far as you could see or smell—" And now, even her voice sounded far away, joyous and free and ecstatic.

The dogs fell to talking about a world without boundary—a world in which they were not subject to the pleasures and displeasures of human beings with their many vagaries and their careless regard for the soul encased in the frame of a dog.

"The more I see of man," concluded Major darkly, "the less I respect the breed."

"I agree with you, Major."

"Sure glad I was born a dog," said Galaxy fervently.

"I'm glad I was born. Period!"

Brandy's remark was greeted by a gale of laughter. Even Blinkie joined in it.

Blinkie loved dogs. They were his friends. He hated people. They were his enemies. The sound of a man's voice never failed to bring resentment into his heart. Blinkie had yet to know kindness at the hands of a master or love in the tone of a man's voice. Although he was only ten months of age, Blinkie had already been acquired and discarded by a bewildering succession of owners. And now, unless Johnson came to claim him, no one would have him—not even as a gift.

Blinkie was different from other dogs. Ever since that accident on Christmas Eve, he had lived in a world that was secret and strange. Only his canine companions were not strangers to him. For in the long months Blinkie had been boarding at Sunnyside, he had come to read the heavy hearts of most of the dogs in the orchard pens.

Insecurity was the troubled bond that tied them to each other.

The sole anchor in Blinkie's life was the old apple tree. It gave him a sense of security to know that at least the old apple tree could not be uprooted, placed in the Sunnyside station wagon and sent into limbo through the great iron gates. But today, even that anchor seemed uncertain and far away.

Golden Boy's bark broke into Blinkie's reverie. "Hey, Blinkie!"

"Yes, Golden Boy?"

"Get on the air waves."

"What is it?"

"I hear a car coming."

"I hear it, too."

"Maybe it's a buyer."

"No, Golden Boy. It's only the butcher."

The excitement subsided, only to start up again. Another car could be heard coming through the entrance gates.

"Who is it this time?"

"Don't know." Blinkie cocked his ears as if to tune up his listening instrument. "No, I don't recognize that one. Never heard that motor before."

"Maybe it's a buyer this time—"

"A buyer!"

"A buyer!"

The magic words spread like a chant. The prospect of a buyer never failed to electrify the atmosphere. A buyer meant home, family life, freedom from the kennel cage. There was no sound more welcome than the song of tires on the concrete road—the approach of voices on the cinder path—the arrival of Parrish with a possible prospect in tow.

The dogs would make a wild dash for the wire mesh marking their enclosures, and hang there pinioned by hope. Which one? Which one would be chosen?

Their thoughts would race. Their hearts would pound. They would stand at attention—breathless spectators to the moving drama of a dog being mated to a master and a master being mated to a dog like a solemn ceremony to which they were the witnesses here in the great cathedral of orchard and sky.

"Sure hope it ain't the butcher or the baker or the gas man again."

"Where's the car heading?"

"It's on its way to the Manor House."

"Maybe it's Julie—"

"No. She drives like velvet."

"Maybe it's Johnson—"

"He doesn't own a car."

"Might be the new manager—"

"No. He's coming in the station wagon. It's a stranger all right," reflected Blinkie. "I never heard that horn before."

"A buyer," mused Trojan longingly. "A buyer is coming here to buy me."

"That's all you ever think about—or dream about—or anything."

"Well, that's the way to make it happen!"

Chorus Girl, the Poodle, wheeled around to regard herself critically. "Wish I had a ribbon on my tail."

"Who'll see you when I'm around?" piped up Hua, the Chihuahua. "I'm imported I'll have you know." She preened. "I'm expensive."

"Nobody's ever gonna buy you, Baby," retorted Gypsy. "I can tell you that right now."

"And why not?"

"You got to be able to spell Chihuahua."

"Yeah. That sure cuts down your chances, Baby!"

Dandy, the Boston Bull, stood up on his back legs, fanned his front paws in the air and burst into poetry:

> "Buyer! Buyer! Come and buy me—
> Anyone would satisfy me!"

"How about it, Blinkie?" Angel was saying. "Wouldn't you like to belong to someone?"

"I've belonged," said Blinkie dully. "I was dropped in a well to drown. I was locked in a store to starve. I was bought for a Christmas present—marked for return. And after what happened that night at the Johnsons'—who would want an old sad sack like me?"

"I like you, Blinkie."

"Thanks, Gala."

"Same here!"

"Me, too!"

There was a strong, reassuring chorus that came at him from all sides.

"Gee whiz, fellers!" Blinkie was embarrassed. "I'm sorry I ever beefed."

"Well, you ain't like the rest of us. You got a legitimate complaint."

"I just wish Rollo would take you—"

"Rollo?" echoed Blinkie. "What's Rollo got to do with it?"

"Well, I heard him talking to Parrish the other day," said Dandy. "Seems like he asked the Boss to give him to you."

"You mean for free?"

"No. He made an offer."

"How much?" demanded Duchess.

"Twenty-five bucks."

"He actually offered to buy me?"

"That's right, Blinkie."

"Well—"

"Well, you know Parrish—"

"Parrish—" disdainfully from Inky. "Don't mention that name to me."

"Don't interrupt. What happened?"

"Parrish turned him down."

"But why?"

"He told Rollo he could not permit any help of his to own a dog."

"That's the rule around here."

"That's the trouble around here. Too many rules."

"Well, he's not in business for love—"

"Dogs may be his business," pronounced Blinkie quietly. "But there's one thing that makes us different from anything else on earth—from sugar or salt—from shoes or hats—from furs or cars or diamond rings." He paused for breath. "Yes, there's one thing they don't know—"

"And what's that?"

"You can buy love," said Blinkie. "Ours is the only love money can buy."

"Brother, you said a mouthful!"

"Yeah. But what are you going to do about it?"

Blinkie did not answer. Instead, he tuned up his ears. In another moment, time would turn in at the entrance gate. As if from far away, he could hear the dogs talking all around him. He could hear the leaves rustling overhead. He could hear his heart beating within his body. And now, in an avalanche of sound drowning out everything else, he could hear the familiar chug of the postman's car on the highway.

It slowed up as usual. Then an odd thing happened. It did not turn in. It did not come up to the mailbox. Instead, it picked up speed and was lost in the maze of other motors. The postman had come and gone—and there had been no letter from Mr. Johnson. Blinkie knew what that meant.

The darkness would be even darker. The world would be even more lonely. The old apple orchard would be no more. He had better say good-by to his friends. Unless a miracle happened, there would be no tomorrow for Blinkie—no morning to follow the night.

But morning came, bringing Rod Morgan with it. He had come to manage Sunnyside. Dogs were his people. He had trained them for war, for work and for leading the blind. Parrish had brought him here to fashion a champ for Westminster.

This was no easy assignment. Rod knew it only too

well. Sweat, skill, meat and money poured into an invisible mold to win the coveted trophy in a game of chance even more speculative than raising horses for horse races.

"I've got one or two dogs I'd like you to see," Parrish was saying as he led the way across the grounds. "Some belong to me, some are boarders and one's a dud on his way out—"

"It takes all kinds of dogs," answered Rod, "just as it does people—"

A playful wind ruffled Rod's thick brown hair. The air was full of bird song. He seemed to be out on a jaunt rather than a work tour of inspection.

"Here we are!" Parrish pointed with his whip. "This is it. The orchard. We grow dogs here." He was trying hard to be facetious. "What do you think of it?"

Rod did not answer. Words could not describe the sight that met his eyes.

An old apple orchard spread out before him, rambling happily up and down hill. The trees in full bloom resembled a parade of plump brides in billowing wedding gowns dancing in the wind.

A good architect must have drawn the design for the place and Nature had done the rest. Here in the orchard were thirteen rows of gleaming white doghouses with thirteen runways in each row. Here in the orchard were individual gardens. Even the paths showed dream and design. A gardener's hand had carefully planted the border walks and trimmed them neatly with seashells.

"Well?" demanded Parrish.

"Why go to heaven? It's right here on earth!"

"People seem to like the idea of leaving their animals here."

"I don't blame them. I bet you have a full house."

"All the time."

"No wonder."

"Yes, this place reassures them."

"You're a pretty smart showman, Parrish. You don't miss a trick."

"I know my business—if that's what you mean."

"I'd like to take a look at the dogs—"

"Go ahead."

Parrish took the lead. As usual, his appearance provoked a chorus of protesting yips and barks. Brandy and Galaxy rushed to their wire enclosures. Duchess and Golden Boy, snarling audibly, crawled back inside their houses. The owner of Sunnyside strode on ahead, his sharp whip, like a teacher's rule, pointing out the lessons.

"We do a brisk trade in boarders, many of them of long standing. The Pointer in the third pen has been here for three years. That Cocker is a newcomer."

"What's the meaning of this?" Rod touched the red ticket fastened to Blinkie's gate. "Is he sold?"

"No. It means he's on his way out."

"Going home?"

"He has no home. I've given orders to destroy him."

"What's he done?"

"It's something that hasn't been done. There's a board bill due on him."

"Been in touch with the owner?"

"We've written him several times but it's no use. He doesn't respond to our letters."

"How long has the dog been here?"

"Four months."

"Anyone who leaves a dog that long without paying up doesn't deserve to get him back."

"I don't want him either. I'm not running a charity ward. Besides, you know the law as well as I do. We're not required to keep an animal beyond the usual thirty days. And this one's not worth keeping."

"Mind if I take a look at him?"

"No. Help yourself."

"What's his name?"

"Blinkie."

"Blinkie!" Rod whistled. He called again. His voice was even softer than his whistle. "Blinkie! Come on, Blinkie! Come on out!"

Blinkie struggled to his feet. He stood on the threshold of his little house in wavering indecision. The strange whistle sounded again. This time, its tone demanded obedience.

"Come on!" ordered Rod. "Here!"

Blinkie came slowly, moving uncertainly in the direction of the strange voice. Then he stood still. Before him was a stranger, a stranger with a new vibration that baffled him. This man was different somehow. The voice was different. The clothes were different. Everything was different.

Rod swooped down and caught Blinkie up in his arms. "Say! What have you got here?"

"A Wire—as you can see for yourself."

"I see he's a Wire. What's more, he happens to be a good one. He has all the makings of a champ."

"Think so?"

Rod went on. "Good stiff wire—the kind I like. His markings are right—the color I like. His tail is short—the length I like. And just look at this head. There's nothing about this dog I don't like, Parrish. I tell you he has the makings of a champ."

"Maybe you'd consider making him a champ?" remarked Parrish lightly. But his tone was devoid of humor.

"Maybe."

"I thought you knew everything there was to know about dogs—"

"Not everything. There isn't a man alive that can't learn something all the time."

"Don't you see what's wrong with the animal?"

"No."

"Take another look, Morgan."

Rod put Blinkie down on the ground and kneeled there beside him. "What's wrong with him?"

"Nothing. Nothing—except that he's blind."

"He's—what?"

"Stone blind. No doubt that's why Johnson deserted him."

"Well, I don't respect him for it. There's a law that's not in the lawbooks. How did it happen?"

So Parrish told Rod the story. He knew what brought Blinkie to Sunnyside.

As Parrish talked, Blinkie found himself caught in the current of the river of time and swept downstream to the source of its flow—the source of remembering from the very beginning when first he had opened his eyes on a world that was breathless with beauty.

Again he saw where he was born—an old red barn that was filled with fragrance. He felt the warm and cuddly bodies of his sisters and brothers. He tasted the flavor of honey on his mother's tongue as she washed his face with kisses.

He came to know the gentle hands of the farmer's wife when she fed him. He grew to love the high frolics in the tall, summer grass, the long days of warm sun, the short nights of deep sleep. And then, suddenly, he was plunged into a cold world ruled by human beings with iron hands.

His first experience taught him pain.

He was given as a gift to a small boy too young to know that a puppy's tail was tender and a puppy's eyes could smart and a puppy's life was in danger when a puppy was dropped down a well.

Blinkie was rescued in the nick of time. He was taken from the small boy and given to the neighborhood grocer.

His second experience taught him fear.

He learned the feel of a stick on his back. He learned the meaning of hunger and thirst and cold. He lived in the dark back room of the grocery store and slept in the damp cellar where the grocery stocks were kept.

At times, he was fed. More often, the grocer forgot to feed him or to free him from the frayed rope by which he was tied to a hot-water pipe. From this vantage point, he was supposed to stand guard over the grocer's goods. But, chained as he was, how could he challenge a burglar?

One day, the grocer sold him to a truck driver. The new buyer tossed him into his truck. He drove Blinkie to a vacant garage. Here was another truck with three other dogs in it. From time to time, other animals were added to the motley collection, until finally there were a dozen dogs crowded in the truck.

Then, one morning, they went on a long, hot ride. They came to the city. It was dusty, noisy, dark. That night, they were dumped unceremoniously into a pet store window.

Here Blinkie stayed, expecting to be happy among half a dozen unhappy puppies of various breeds and dispositions. Morley, the pet store proprietor, was very temperamental. One day, he would shower them with kindness.

The next day would find him harsh, coarse, irritable. He had dogs for sale and he could not sell them quickly enough.

The one thing that intrigued Blinkie was the street outside the window. Here was a banquet for the eye. All day long, the feast went on in a steady parade of faces. All sorts of people, old and young, ugly and beautiful, happy and sad, came to the window to look at the pets. Some of the faces were starved with yearning. Some of the eyes were dark with grief yet lighted up briefly at the antics of the puppies in the window. People could be nice, decided Blinkie.

The month was December. He heard Morley talk about the approaching holidays.

Christmas was in the air, pungent with pine and bay-berry. Morley bustled about, decorating the shop. He unrolled the crêpe paper streamers and strung them in crosses from the ceiling. He hung a great green wreath on the door. He wrote gilded words of good cheer across the stained and faded mirrors. He bubbled over with the holiday spirit. Christmas meant a brisk business for the pet shop. The sale of dogs at holiday time was usually very good.

All through the week—one by one—the puppies were lifted out of the window by Morley and put through their awkward paces in front of prospective buyers. One by one, Blinkie's companions were purchased as Christmas presents, outfitted with new leashes and trotted proudly out the door.

The day of Christmas Eve saw only one dog left in the window to tempt the passing public. Blinkie alone remained to sit in the lumpy sawdust like Cinderella relegated to the ashes of a deserted hearth. One or two people dropped in to price him. But nobody offered to buy him and give him a home.

The day began moving into dusk. All at once, the world grew gray, darkened beyond the hour. All at once, an unexpected flurry of soft, thick snow filled the air. All at once, it was almost night even though the hour was early.

Christmas Eve came down in a rush from the swollen, winter sky. Morley peered out of the window into the heart of the storm. He frowned at Blinkie, counted his cash, and began to close down his shop. He reached for his coat and hat. He reached for his key. He moved toward the door.

Blinkie knew just what to expect. The lights would go out. Then darkness would come on, darkness and cold and loneliness.

Suddenly, the doorbell tinkled—and there stood Mr. Johnson.

Things happened swiftly after that, more swiftly than Blinkie cared to remember. Mr. Johnson bought him. He was placed on the floor between the counters and outfitted with a new leash and collar. He was measured for a brand-new dog valise. Then Mr. Johnson purchased a box of dog tidbits and pocketed his change. The doorbell tinkled behind them. Blinkie stood outside. He was free. He drew his first breath of freedom—and it tasted delicious.

They walked for quite a while. The snow was delicious, too. There was taste in everything, it seemed, in the world around him and in the world within him. Even his thoughts tasted good. He was going home. He was going home—at last!

The streets were electric with cold, a good cold that pinched his warm paws. Strangers whistled in greeting and he yipped back with joy. A lady stooped down to pat him. He stood very still till she finished. Mr. Johnson flagged a taxicab. Blinkie found himself riding in style, seated beside his new master on the back seat. It was all he could do to keep his balance but somehow he managed to do it.

All the way there, he wondered what sort of home, what sort of people he was going to meet. Any children? What sort of house? A garden maybe? A homey farm with woods beyond it?

The house proved disappointing.

They climbed four flights of stairs to a cluttered city apartment. A mob of shrieking children greeted him at the threshold. Children seemed to be everywhere. They pulled his ears. They tweaked his tail. They stepped on his sensitive toes. They tried to ride him like a horse. They brought him food that was cold and dry. They forgot to bring him water.

Finally, Mrs. Johnson came home from a shopping spree. She dropped her packages at the sight of Blinkie.

"A dog!" she shrieked, her eyes full of ire at Mr. Johnson. "A dog!" she advanced on Blinkie. "What is the meaning of this?"

"He's a Christmas present," said Mr. Johnson.

"A Christmas present? I need a new dress. And what do you bring me? A *dog* for Christmas!"

"I'll put him in the kitchen."

"No, Pop!" the children clamored. "Leave him right here—right here under the tree."

What happened in the hours that followed was something Blinkie had since tried his desperate best to forget. Yet how could he forget the cruel treatment that followed? They placed him under the tree along with the other presents. But he was a present that was going back. He was a purchase that was marked for return.

The night was a nightmare. The room kept filling with noise and confusion. The children began running around the tree, chasing each other in a game of tag. They paid no attention to their father's command to stop. Mrs. Johnson was too angry to care. She stayed in the kitchen, clattering the supper dishes.

No one knew how it happened.

It may have been a faulty connection. Perhaps one of the boys pulled a wire that was loose.

There was the flash of spark. It ran up the trunk of the tree like a vein of lightning. In less than a minute—without any warning—the pine needles spurted into flame. In an instant—all of it—the tree—the decorations—the gifts and the wrappings—were one big geyser of bright red fire.

Blinkie struggled to free himself. But the leash with which they had fastened him seemed to grow tighter instead—bringing him closer and closer to the crimson flare.

He could smell the pungent scent of blazing pine. He could feel the burning branches as they set his body on fire. He could hear voices. Then the voices died out. The light died out. It stayed out. The fire was gone. There was only oblivion all about him—a sea of warm, gray kind oblivion.

Now he could hear Mr. Johnson's voice as if from a distance. The voice came closer. The words became clearer.

"How is he, Doc?"

"Seems to be coming around."

"That's good!"

"I've never seen such a fighter."

"This dog sure has guts."

"Yes, he's pulling out of it, slow but sure. Looks to me like he'll make it."

"Congrats!"

"Not so fast, Mr. Johnson. I have bad news for you—"

"What is it, Doc?"

"He'll never be the same again."

"Why not?"

"I'm afraid he's going to be blind."

"Blind?" Mr. Johnson seemed stunned.

Blinkie's heart missed a beat. He blinked his eyes and lay there wishing he had never come out of that deep sea of oblivion.

"Look, Doc. His eyes are wide open—"

"That's right. Wide open. Just the same, he can't see. He'll never be able to see—not any more, Mr. Johnson. You're lucky he's still alive."

"What'll I do now? I can't take him back to the store where I bought him. I can't take him home. My wife doesn't want him. I can't take him with me. I'm leaving for the road. As a matter of fact, I'm already late getting down to New Orleans. When you're a traveling man, Doc, your time isn't your own. You're given an itinerary and you reach your customers on schedule—or else. You—"

"But what about the dog?"

"Say! How about boarding him with you?"

"Sorry. I don't board animals."

Mr. Johnson was deflated. "Now what? Dogs are out of my line. I never owned one before. Maybe you know of some place I could take him. Maybe some kennel would keep him for me."

"Why not try Sunnyside? You couldn't find a better place to board him. You can tell Parrish I sent you. I only hope they take him in—"

And so Johnson had brought Blinkie to Sunnyside.

Blinkie followed every word with avid attention as Parrish recounted all this to Rod. Some of it Parrish knew. Some of it he could only guess. Some of it went untold, for only Blinkie had lived through the fear and the horror and the terror and the turmoil of the past.

The telling was over. Parrish emptied his pipe, hitting it hard against Blinkie's little white doghouse. The dead ashes dropped to the ground. A dead silence followed.

"And I haven't seen Johnson since," concluded Parrish. "So we'll have to get rid of the dog."

Rod's voice sounded cold as ice. He stood up, holding Blinkie safe in the strong crook of his arms, almost in a gesture of defiance aimed at Parrish.

"I'll make a deal with you—"

"What is it?"

"I'll pay his bill. What's more, I'll buy this dog from you."

"He's yours," said Parrish with a flip of his whip. "But what good is he to you? He's blind—"

"So was I," answered Rod. "They gave me a guide dog at Morristown. Then the doctors operated and I got back my sight." He grinned. "Maybe something could be done for Blinkie. Meanwhile, he'll be my dog—and I'll be his Seeing-Eye guy!"

The Lost Dog Brings a Gift

by Anne Elizabeth Wilson

MR. PRANDELLO and his horse-drawn merry-go-round were on their southern journey. By Christmas he hoped to reach a little town where the sun always led him home. He and Juan, the monkey, both felt the cold these autumn days. As for Vicky, their White West Highland Terrier, she seemed to love the late fall weather, and often, much to their dismay, went for long hunts along the country roads, chasing rabbits and digging after field mice.

On the days when she left them to scamper along in the fields, Juan was very unhappy. Sometimes he was able to keep up with her by running along the fences, but when she began digging it bored him, and he got cold waiting for her. He understood trees and rails to swing on, but to dig—it was then he realized that, after all, she was a dog and he only a little old monkey with rheumatism. Yet at night, when they cuddled up together in the bottom of the wagon, and she kept him warm in her wiry fur, he forgot the difference between them and only remembered that she was the dearest thing in his life. He was no longer lonely or worried, with his arms about her neck and her cold nose under his ear.

"Ah, Veecky," Mr. Prandello told her one night as he handed her a hamburger sandwich for her supper, "you are getting to be a beeg girl, but you are young yet. Juan and me, we get older everee day, and you only grow up. Sometime you forget we are ole man, eh?"

Juan looked at him, worried again. There was something in his voice that seemed to be scolding Vicky. He sidled up to her and put his arm around her protectingly.

"You are right!" approved Mr. Prandello. "You take care of her. She a beeg girl now."

It was true. Vicky's fur had reached its full lovely growth, and the happiness and freedom of life with Mr. Prandello and Juan, always in the open, always playing with the children, had made her a handsome dog. Her small sharp ears stood up on her shaggy head like two spikes in a white chrysanthemum. Juan loved to press them down and watch them spring up again. Her whiskers were fluffy about a jet-black shiny nose, and her black claws a perfect outline about the edge of her rough white paws. People often asked Mr. Prandello where she came from, but he always laughed and looked at Juan.

"Ask heem," he would chuckle, and the story of how she came to them out of a broken window would flicker across Mr. Prandello's mind with a little tug of remorse

for the mistress she had forgotten, to follow the sunshine
up and down with them.

So on they went through the little towns where the
sunshine still held, looking toward Christmas. It was
one day in October as they were trundling along a soft old
dirt road that seemed to help Chiquita's pavement-sore
feet, that Vicky suddenly bounced off the seat beside
Mr. Prandello and disappeared through a fence so
quickly that Juan had no time to run after her. He tugged
at Mr. Prandello to stop Chiquita, but his master was
asleep with the reins tied about the whip. He chattered
and cried, but Chiquita plodded on, and in the sharp

wind, he was afraid to run off and search alone. What if he should be left there on the cold road and the wagon miles ahead? What if Vicky never found him, either? He knew how she ran like a hare through the grass and forgot everything in some foolish woodchuck hole. What should he do? He finally decided, monkey-like, to bury his anxiety in Mr. Prandello's vest. It was at least warm there. They were not going fast—surely Vicky would come out of the bushes a little farther on and Chiquita would stop for her. He tried to comfort himself under Mr. Prandello's arm, and finally went to sleep, too.

It was evening when Chiquita came to a stop at a crossroad and waited for some sign to guide her. The stopping of the wagon awoke Mr. Prandello and he stretched comfortably.

"Come, Juan," called Mr. Prandello. "Come, Veecky," he yawned, "we mus' light the lantern."

Juan chattered at the cold that reached him as Mr. Prandello moved, and he felt about the seat for Vicky to keep him warm—then he remembered. She had left them to play, and they had deserted her! Reaching up for Mr. Prandello's suspenders, he shook them furiously. For a moment, he thought he would die if he could not speak. She was gone!

"Juan, you are crazee?" scolded Mr. Prandello. "Where is Veecky—she will play with you. I am beezy now."

Juan was beside himself. It was like that day when Vicky sat crying behind the closed window, and he had to break the pane to let her out—when he could not bear for Mr. Prandello to go away and leave her.

"Juan!" Mr. Prandello picked him up and looked about the seat and on the floor of the wagon. "Where is Veecky?"

Juan shrieked. Where *was* Vicky? He could only hide his head against Mr. Prandello and wail.

"You bad monkey!" Mr. Prandello said most unjustly. "Why you no tell me? She is lost herself, you know. She's go 'way, an' I tole you mus' look after her now." He shook Juan to ease his own worry, and they both sat down and looked at each other despairingly.

"We have to go back."

It is hard to describe that night—how for hours, in the chill October wind, they stumbled up and down the road, calling, searching, asking at unfriendly doors for a word of a little white dog with a shiny black nose. Country people are suspicious of old men with wagons in the night—it is not like a city street where all the children know and love him for the merry-go-round.

At dawn, Mr. Prandello tethered Chiquita under a tree and built a little fire where he and Juan sat in silent misery.

"You and me are very ole man," he told the monkey sadly. "She was jes young girl. Maybe she know better how to get along."

Juan was exhausted. He had fallen asleep, holding on to Mr. Prandello's braces. His master wrapped his coat around him and lay down by the fire. When the sun came out, they would have to go on to the next town. Money must be made to see them on their way, and if they did well, perhaps they could stay awhile and come back for her again.

They stayed a week in that town, but Juan could not bear to play with the children now. There was no heart in anything. He sat hunched up on Mr. Prandello's shoulder and let his cup swing on its chain, for he seemed not to have the strength even to hold it. Mr. Prandello had to take the five-cent pieces and pennies, and he made lots of mistakes in change. The policeman made him move from one place to another so fast that he could never get in his final and best ride—the one where he always made the most money. But late in the afternoon, he always hurried out to the country again, searching dispiritedly, calling, hoping. The farmers began to know him and offered him night lodging in their barns occasionally, and sometimes supper. Once or twice he played the hurdy-gurdy and ran the merry-go-round as a treat for the country children, but Vicky could not have heard it, for she never came.

Then it was that Juan fell really ill. He would not eat, and the ever-chilling air seemed to paralyze him. Mr. Prandello knew that he must hurry after the sunshine if he were to save his life. In a little heap of misery, the monkey clung to Chiquita's blanket on the bottom of the seat, crying like a sick baby. Once or twice, at the sound of a dog's bark on the street, he seemed to come to life for a moment, looking about excitedly—only to fall back again into the stupor that had at last overtaken him.

Heartsick, Mr. Prandello decided that they must press on. Some mothers forbade their children to go near the wagon with a sick monkey in it now—who knew what he might give them? Alas, who knew? Watching him,

Mr. Prandello felt that he too would soon come down with the illness if he could not save Juan.

There was a little place not far away that he remembered, where there was a good man who looked after sick animals. He once had cured Juan when he nearly died after a fall—perhaps he could help him now. But Juan was lying so still when they came to the doctor's door, that when he looked at him he shook his head.

"This little fellow," he told Mr. Prandello, "is dying. It looks to me like a case of pining. They often go that way. Has he lost his mate?"

"Me—heem—we have no mate," laughed Mr. Prandello sadly, "only a friend—leedle white dog. She go away."

"Well, you might replace her. What was she like?"

Again Mr. Prandello went into his pathetic description of Vicky, growing more excited over her wiry white coat, her black nose and bushy whiskers as he went along.

"Well, well," smiled the doctor, "she must have been a beautiful dog. Did she look anything like this?" He held up a card with a picture on it. "There's a kennel of these dogs near here. You'll have to get him another, although I doubt if they have anything as fine as the one you lost. Still, it might save the monkey."

"Maria!" exclaimed Mr. Prandello, almost in tears as he looked at the card, "eet ees her seester! How much to buy?"

"Oh, I'll get you one quite cheap, when they know how badly you need one. Come along, we'll take the monkey and see how he feels about a new pal."

The kennel owner was very sympathetic. He took Mr.

Prandello and Juan into a comfortable long house where dozens of little white heads and black noses looked up at them from behind wire-covered pens—then suddenly there was one sharp, unbelievable bark. Juan thrust his face out of Mr. Prandello's coat with his eyes nearly popping out of his head; his claw-like little hands clutched frantically in the air—he leapt.

"It's a cure," laughed the doctor.

"Ees a miracle," Mr. Prandello corrected him.

"Here, here," protested the kennel owner, for Juan had seemingly gone mad. He had climbed into one of the pens and was half choking one of the white dogs to death.

The doctor was more concerned for Mr. Prandello, for he was shaking with some emotion that neither of the men could understand. Torrents of Spanish poured from his very heart. At least they believed that he wanted to pay them some money. He was emptying small change all over the floor.

"You don't know—you don't know!" he stammered, slowing down into English. "Eet ees Veecky—hees friend. *He ees find hees friend!*"

The doctor and the kennel owner looked away. "Certainly he can have her," the owner told him. "Some children brought her to me, thinking she was one of mine. They said she had followed them. I was glad to have her, for she's a fine dog, but there's no doubt she belongs to that monkey!"

Oh no, there was no doubt. Among the wildest clamor, with every dog in the kennel barking and jumping, Vicky and Juan were rolling over and over in the straw. Finally she held him down with one paw and sniffed his poor little skeleton of a body from head to toe. Then she licked his face until he had to shut his eyes and gasp for breath. At last, he put his arms about her neck and broke into such weeping that Mr. Prandello had to speak to him.

"He's not going to die when he holler lak dat, eh?" he asked the doctor proudly. "He very ole man, but he goin' leeve maybe a hundred—hah?"

"I wouldn't be surprised," grinned the doctor. "He's all right now, anyway."

The sun was growing brighter every day, and Juan was hungry for the fruit along the way. He was even beginning to grow a little fatter. Vicky was more beautiful than ever. Mr. Prandello thought he had never seen her look so handsome. She never wanted to run after rabbits these warm days, but sat up in a very dignified way as

they joggled along. The bright weather made her sleepy, and sometimes she closed her eyes in pure contentment.

"Veecky, Veecky," Mr. Prandello told her then, "soon we come to my church where I can burn candle to thank for you come back to Juan and me." He was speaking of the little town which he thought of most as home since he had left South America, where it was always like a summer day and many people still spoke Spanish though it was no longer a Spanish country. It was near here that men once searched for a Fountain of Youth, and Juan and Chiquita and Mr. Prandello felt years fall away from their bones whenever they reached it.

There Chiquita would be loosed from the harness, to drowse and grow fat in a cozy stable, and Juan could pretend he was a little jungle monkey once more in the palm trees about the house. For Mr. Prandello's brother was an important man and owned a fine piece of land. He had set Mr. Prandello up in business with the merry-go-round. Someday, when Juan and Chiquita were too old to follow the summer up and down any more, they would all come there to rest in the sun, and the merry-go-round would stay in the garden of the good parish priest, Padre Humberto, for good.

It was such a fine lazy place there. Mr. Prandello and his little nephew, Manuel, would spend a whole week repainting the animals in the wagon, for instance. The swan's wings would have a coat of white, his bill of glossy black. There would be a new cushion between his wings, and fresh harness for all the other animals. Manuel always thought the tiger was the best to paint, orange and black stripes—unless it was the touch of silver and gold on the bits and bridles.

Because his brother was such a good businessman, he always made Mr. Prandello put any money he still had in the bank, but because Mr. Prandello was even a better businessman, he always used to have a little bag of coins left over. Those were for Padre Humberto, to use for the children of the parish for Christmas. "The children give it to me—I give it to them," he always explained. It was sound common sense. And on Christmas Eve when the merry-go-round was all painted new, it played and ran all day in the Padre's garden.

Perhaps you cannot imagine a Christmas where flowers tumble down over white walls and birds sing the most piercing sweet song, but that was the only one which Juan and Mr. Prandello knew. For them, it was the dearest summer of all the year. And now to Vicky, napping on the wagon seat, it seemed that all the drowsiest scents in the world were folding about her.

So she dreamed along until that day when they drew up before a small white house with green palmettos about it, and there was excitement enough for everyone. Juan had begun to wake up miles away, dashing from saddle to saddle in the back of the wagon. Then just when they rounded his brother's lane, Mr. Prandello set the hurdy-gurdy going, and people began rushing out-of-doors like bees from a hive.

At first Vicky was frightened, but when a big woman with soft eyes picked her up in her arms and began kissing her (everybody was kissing everybody else), she realized that it was going to be all right. It was Mr. Prandello's sister-in-law, Lucia. Juan had disappeared in the midst of arms and heads, and Mr. Prandello and his brother were dancing, holding each other around the waist, hitting each other on the back, and knocking each other's hats off. Vicky was afraid for a moment that Mr. Prandello was getting hurt, but they finally began kissing each other, too.

Yet when it was all over, and Chiquita was led to the stable, Vicky was not sorry, for she felt a little bewildered. She was glad to find a box of clean straw in Chiquita's stall where she could curl up and wait for Juan. She knew he would find her soon. She could hear voices coming from the house, and she knew that, anyway, Mr. Prandello was safe and happy. But it was toward morning that Juan finally climbed in beside her. His little heart was still beating fast, for he had had a very gay time. Everyone was so busy that they had forgotten to take his tin cup off. Vicky nosed it out of the way, licked his eyes, and placing one paw over his chest in a motherly way, sighed and went to sleep again. It was so good to have a real bed of their own once more.

Christmas Eve came very soon, and the wagon, all resplendent in its new paint, was driven to Padre Humberto's garden for the children's party. Mr. Prandello and Manuel had permission to take Vicky and Juan to the chapel in order to burn a candle in thanksgiving for their safe return. He showed them the little manger by the altar where a smiling Baby lay with outstretched arms, and statues of oxen, cows, and sheep stood watching over Him. It was the crèche of the Christ Child, and Padre

Humberto was willing for Vicky and Juan to be shown it, for was it not true that dumb creatures were among the first to worship at the manger on the first Christmas?

"It is the holy Bambino," Mr. Prandello told them. "Is He not a beautiful Child?" He knelt by the crèche, and with Juan on his shoulder, lifted Vicky up to see it more closely. They were both very quiet and good, and Juan, seeing that Manuel and Mr. Prandello were bareheaded, took his hat off too.

"He love all leetle dog and monkey," whispered Mr. Prandello as he went down on his knees on the way out, and glancing around to see that no one was looking, sprinkled a little holy water over them both at the fountain.

That night, Juan and Vicky were alone in the stable with Chiquita. For some reason, Vicky would not leave her box, nor would she allow Juan to get in beside her, but growled at him strangely. He sat disconsolately on Chiquita's back, watching her and thinking. In spite of all the happiness and blessing of the day, he felt a certain sadness, and it was made sharper by Vicky's unfriendliness.

He began thinking how it would be a little later on in the house, when, after midnight mass, the family would bring Padre Humberto back to supper. How the tree would be lighted, and Lucia would play on the guitar. Then they would all give each other presents, and he knew there would surely be one for him, one for Vicky, one for Chiquita. Yet he knew that in all the years he had shared Christmas with human beings he had never been happy, although he had never been forgotten. Was it possible that it was because, of all those gathered there, he was the only one who never had anything to give?

He went back to the box to try to tell Vicky his thoughts, but she would not listen to him. She was so different tonight, growling softly and nosing away the straw into a little round nest.

At last, lonely and perplexed, he decided he would go into the house and try to have some fun with Manuel. He knew there would be great doings in the parlor by now.

Yes, they had already begun giving each other things.

"For you, Padre!" announced Lucia, in Spanish, handing the priest a large white box. He opened it with eyes rolled heavenward in protest against such extravagance. It was a new black pancake hat!

"Ah, no, Padre, do not scold. You disgrace your cloth with what you would wear if we did not clothe you. Did I not see your best shoes today on the big feet of that worthless husband of Maria Cortez? But it would be a brave man who would wear the Padre's *hat*—at least you cannot give this away. . . ."

Juan listened and watched, and between the two it seemed that there was more happiness in Lucia's face as she gave the gift than in the Padre's as he took it. How could she blame the Padre if in turn he gave things away?

When they handed him his own package off the tree, Juan was delighted as he importantly tore the paper off, to find that it was a little hat very much like the Padre's. From the clink inside Chiquita's package he knew it was a big new bell, and from the feel of Vicky's, he knew it was a new collar.

"But where is she?" demanded Lucia in Spanish. "The little dog is not here to receive her present."

"Ah," said the Padre, who seemed to know animals so well that he could read their very thoughts, Juan believed, "she is just making ready her own Christmas gift. Today in the chapel she spoke to me of something she was preparing for her master."

What was this? Vicky preparing a gift and not to tell him? Juan was bitter. So it was perhaps because of this she would not let him in the box—she was hiding it from him!

"Yes," went on the Padre, "a gift has been prepared for this Christmas feast by the dumb creatures who live in the stable. Shall we go now and exchange our presents there?"

"You are making riddles, Padre," chided Mr. Prandello. "Is it some more of your foolish generosity?"

"Surely not mine," smiled the priest. "Am I to blame if the Good Lord sees fit to bless this house?"

They lit the lantern and Padre Humberto led the way. "Walk softly," he warned them, "she may not be quite ready to receive us."

But Juan could not be held back. He rushed ahead and was balanced on Chiquita's stall with his hand over his heart, preparing to make the most sweeping bow in his life. Oh, he knew it now—he knew the feeling that had made Lucia's eyes so bright when she gave the Padre his hat; the reason why the Padre himself gave his shoes away; the thing within them that made people sing and

act like children. Here in the stable, they, too, had something to give. . . .

"A little more light, my friend," said the Padre holding
the lantern over the stall. "Ah, there is your gift. . . ."

It lay in Vicky's box—a little white package making
sounds like a toy mouse from a Christmas stocking. Its
tiny ears and eyes were sealed, as all good presents should
be, and its nose and toes were almost as red as a poinset-
tia.

"*Madre de Dios!*" said Mr. Prandello in a hushed voice,
"it is—it is . . ."

"It is—a bambino," laughed Padre Humberto.

Chiquita put her head down and sniffed softly at the
puppy. Vicky lifted her fluffy face and looked at them
proudly.

"From us!" shouted Juan in his heart, almost fainting
with joy. He made one tremendous bow after another,
until quite dizzy, but perfectly happy, he fell over back-
wards into the straw and lay looking up into their faces.
He thought he saw something there that he had not noticed even in the parlor.

So it was that Mr. Prandello received his Christmas
gift.

Choirboy

by Paul Annixter

OUR TOWN OF BAYSPORT had made quite a memorable showing for its size in World War I. But in World War II we didn't seem to run to heroes. A lot of us went across and we saw more rugged going, in stretches, than was dreamed of at Château-Thierry and the Marne, but none of us hit the glory trail. Young Corey Boynton came the nearest of any and he returned with only some hash marks and a rocker on his sleeve and a military citation. But we had our war hero all the same—Choirboy, old Jesse Hunnicutt's favorite dog.

Jesse was one of the greatest hunters and dog trainers this country has even known. He had raised Choirboy from a pup, had been his trainer and almost constant companion for four years, before he was brought to bed with his last illness. Choirboy broke all the rules Jesse had set up for hunting dogs. He wasn't even purebred, and people used to rib Jesse unmercifully about it. Jesse called him a Walker, but the dog had in him, of all things,

43

a mixture of mastiff that was discernible to the schooled eye. The result was a heavy, seamed and melancholy face, big bones and great lubberly paws, the heart of a lion and a world of wisdom and forbearance in his steady tawny depth of eye.

Choirboy was named for the peculiar musical cadence of his trail song when hunting fox or rabbits in the hills, which was sometimes high and wild and clear and again would drop to a deep and mellow gong note. He was slow, but tenacious, and the surest, coldest-nosed dog Jesse ever had.

When the call had gone out for dogs to join the K-9 Corps, Choirboy with his intensive training had been one of the eligibles in Baysport. And Jesse himself, although it almost broke his heart, wanted Choirboy to go. The two had hunted their last hunt together. Jesse knew it, but Choirboy didn't. That was the tough part of it. For months the dog had been languishing miserably, unable to understand why Jesse never went any more to the woods and fields they both loved. It had been hard on both of them, for Choirboy was a one-man dog and Jesse was very close to being a one-dog man.

"You'd best sign him up if they'll take him, Liddy," Jesse had told his wife. "He's eating his heart out here, and anyway there ought to be one Hunnicutt in this man's war."

So Choirboy was drafted into the K-9 Corps and put into a commando outfit, for he was of the heavy-muscled, one-track, shock-troop kind. What he went through before they made a killer out of him must have gone beyond all telling. He had been one of the first dogs to land in the islands and he had made a great record for himself and Baysport, down there in the jungles. But this story is to deal purely with his postwar record.

It was in '45 that Choirboy came home with three neat chevrons and a rocker shaved carefully in the fur of his right foreleg—and the Purple Heart! He'd served a year and a half, seen action in three of the grimmest of our Pacific island pushes. And what action! He'd got the Purple Heart when he was wounded while slipping through a cordon of Japs by night, where no human could have won through, carrying a message that brought reinforcements and victory.

They'd spent a long time rehabilitating the killer out of him before his release—an impossible task in many cases, but Choirboy's great heart and intrinsic kindliness had won out over the mayhem machine into which he'd been transformed. In spite of all he'd been through he was never vicious and he was always a friend to children. But old Jesse Hunnicutt in the meantime had died; his wife had left our town, and so it was Jesse's brother, Ed Hunnicutt, who came by the dog. Ed paid for the dog's keep and his collars—Choirboy didn't have to have a license in our town any more; our mayor had proclaimed that publicly. For there was the matter of the Purple Heart and the whole town regarded the dog as precious civic property, though Ed Hunnicutt was his legal owner.

Ed, who managed the town bank, was a grand fellow, though no hunter or outdoor man. It was for that reason, I always felt, that Choirboy never really cottoned to him. That was a real grief to Ed, though he didn't talk about it. For Ed really loved the dog and was proud as Punch over his war record. He talked of him fondly and a bit wistfully as "my dog," but Choirboy never belonged to him in that special sense in which a dog is supposed to be a man's, and he seldom stayed at Ed's place. It was just a point of call among scores of others.

No man, I knew, would ever "own" Choirboy again, but I think that I came closer than anyone to taking Jesse Hunnicutt's place with him. I didn't own any part of him, but he and I had a tie. We'd known each other a long time and to Choirboy I was the last link to the good old life that was all but forgotten. I'd been one of Jesse's closest friends, you see, and dozens of times the three of us had hunted together through the fall woods.

The very first day Choirboy was back in town he checked up on me in the old *Baysport Banner* building where I've been combined police, society and sports reporter and pinch-hit columnist for fifteen years. I heard the rattle of his worn nails along the corridor, then into the office he burst, to rear up and fling his great forepaws against my chest and give me the dangdest look a dog ever gave a man. A look of swift joy and eagerness and hope, followed by question, suspicion.

Finally a sort of confusion came over him when he failed to get the special news he wanted. His tail went dead in its socket, the eager light died out of his eyes and a look of dull disappointment fell over his seamed face. He was seeking rumor of Jesse Hunnicutt in the place he'd been surest of it, and finding none. And there was nothing I could do to bridge the silent gulf between us. It was enough to break your heart.

From that time on Choirboy never missed a day in look-

ing in on me. He'd always had free run of the *Banner* building and about ten each morning I'd hear him padding down the corridor. We'd pass the time of day, he'd give me that deep imploring look, then leave to continue his search.

His days came to consist of one endless round of the town's stores, bars and restaurants and the many homes where he was known and loved. From the day of his return the town had had to reckon with him in a general municipal sense. And soon Choirboy had to reckon with the town, in ways not all to the good. Everywhere he went he was greeted, coddled and given outrageous handouts of food. At the butcher shops they saved heart and liver for him, which he liked; there was cake forthcoming at the bakeries, fish at the harbor, and candy at the sweetshops if he'd have it. Wherever he deigned to stop, a meal and a welcome awaited him. As in the case with many a human hero, his home town was doing its unconscious best to make a vag and a softy out of him.

As a result, Choirboy began taking on layers of fat beneath his sleek coat where no fat should be, and a certain dullness of satiety clouded his fine topaz eyes. But though he succumbed to the fleshpots he wasn't happy. There was always a depth of sadness and yearning in his lined face and his spirit seemed often afar. He was still engaged in his quest for Jesse Hunnicutt in all these peregrinations, hopeless and hollow though it was; but as the many months went by, the very object of his search dimmed to the vanishing point, as it does with animals, so that in time it was mere force of habit that drove him on.

Two propensities the Army had given him. The first was an overweening love of numbers. Wherever five or more people were in congregation, there Choirboy was to be found. No band concert, fire, park picnic or club conclave went ungraced by his presence.

People, particularly men, were his meat, although he was also honorary member, professional greeter and, alas, official cake-and-pie taster of our Ladies' Aid Society.

The second propensity was an ingrained distrust and hatred of firearms. One fine morning Walnut Street was thrown into considerable hubbub when Choirboy spotted little Ferdie Hyatt firing a noisy cap pistol in a game of war with another boy. On an impulse Ferdie turned his pistol on Choirboy. Although belligerence had been quite trained out of the dog, a pistol was a pistol, a thing of evil and of the enemy. For a moment he must have forgotten himself, for Ferdie got the fright of his life as a bristling yellow-eyed demon suddenly challenged him with a voice like water sucking down a big drain. The prompt appearance of a policeman brought Choirboy back to Baysport and the present; or rather, I think, the sight of the patrolman's uniform, for the dog had brought back a lasting respect for regimentals.

These doings of Choirboy's furnished me with the meatiest sort of copy. Not a week went by but a boxed story appeared on the front page, which our delighted citizenry came to watch for each new misadventure of the town's pampered anachronism. An Army magazine reprinted these and wrote Choirboy up.

Although the dog continued to operate ostensibly out of the old farmhouse he had come home to, under the aegis of Ed Hunnicutt, he and Ed had less and less to do with each other. There just wasn't any companionship there, no gearing-in, Ed being the quiet indoor man he was. If Ed called the dog, for instance, and he felt like coming, he'd come; if he didn't, he wouldn't. Ed never even got to groom him and I was the one who kept Choirboy's chevrons neatly trimmed—a matter of pride.

It got so he rarely spent a night at Ed's place; he much preferred the company of one or other of the town's night patrolmen on their rounds, or mixing with the crowds in the railroad depot; or if I happened to be working late, to lie beside my desk, one eye shut and the other blinking at me if I so much as stirred a foot. Sometimes I'd try to make him spend the night at my rooms, but Army life had given him a sort of claustrophobia. After half an hour he'd give the door an apologetic thump and take his leave.

When fall came I managed to take him hunting with me once a week. But our afternoons afield turned out to be sad affairs. Both of us had begun to feel the years. My heart wasn't in it any more and that Epicurean girth Choirboy had taken on was no help at all to flashy field work. We simply went through the strict formalities of the hunt, never a point missed or slurred over on Choirboy's part; we'd shoot a bird or two without verve, without pleasure, both our minds harking back to other days and other hunts when old Jesse had been along. It was too depressing and before long I gave it up.

The days and weeks went by, a whole year and a half of them. The town jogged peacefully along; the *Banner* editions came out on unvarying schedule.

And Choirboy's weird doings were also unvarying. His great love had been distilled through time and pain, and war and death, into the love of many, so that now he was no man's dog, or everyman's dog, as you like. His restlessness and that growing gregariousness had had their way and he was by now, in every sense except verbal oath, a full-fledged Moose, an Elk, an Odd Fellow, a Woodman of the World with a passion for evening drill, an American Legionnaire and an enthusiastic member of our Commercial Club, with a clean record of never a meeting missed.

He also lent his unwavering support to all band concerts, marriages, dances—and even funerals, where he reflected the spirit of the occasion and lay pensive with his head beneath a chair, even moaning miserably on one or two occasions. So fervent a rooter had he become for the Baysport baseball team that a special player had to be detailed to keep him from lolloping over the diamond when a game was in progress.

But he was going the way of most returned heroes by now; there was a definite sag to his fuselage, and he was softening, slipping downgrade—a tame and civic institution, so taken for granted that his glorious record afield had practically become a myth. And to become a myth while still alive is to sit in the ash heap indeed. It looked like the curtain had gone down on the second and last act of Choirboy's drama.

Then one Saturday morning it went up suddenly on a surprise third act. It was near eleven o'clock and Choirboy had looked in at the Citizens' Bank to check up on Ed Hunnicutt, for after all Ed had been closer to Jesse than most. Ed was at his usual desk in the little railed-in front office, signing up a workman for a loan, when Choirboy reared up with a yawping sound of greeting, resting his big front feet on the oak counter. Ed looked up, sort of pleased as he always was at sight of the dog, but he ordered Choirboy to get down. I heard it, for I was in line at the teller's window with a pay check.

Choirboy was turning disconsolately toward the door when into the bank strode two young men, Mace Turner, of Winslow, Arizona, and Juan Bacca, of Socorro, New Mexico, names well known to the marshals of five states and numerous FBI agents, as we later learned. Turner wore gloves; Bacca wore a Colt automatic, which he immediately produced, ordering the bank personnel and the nine amazed customers to reach for the ceiling.

Turner vaulted the oak counter into Ed Hunnicutt's office and thence into the tellers' cages where he scooped all available money into a leather case.

"Everybody into the vault," Turner ordered. "Step lively now and nobody'll get hurt."

He, too, had a Colt in his hand now. We customers and the entire bank force, with hands raised, began a slow shuffle toward the rear of the bank where the heavy vault door stood open. It was like a scene from an old silent movie. Choirboy still stood uncertainly in the middle of the floor, watching proceedings with mixed wonder and suspicion. Guns. He didn't like them. He wasn't liking any of it, it was plain; but everyone had forgotten Choirboy apparently.

Everyone, that is, but Ed Hunnicutt and me. I looked at Ed's pale strained face and saw his glance fix on Choirboy, and in that swift suspended moment I read his mind, got the overtone of it, or harmonic, you might say. Choirboy, too, was looking at Ed. He'd begun to bristle.

"Get him, boy!" came Ed's sudden sharp order, his finger pointing at Bacca in the center of the floor with his menacing gun. In the same instant Ed dropped from sight behind the oak counter.

I saw Choirboy, a snarling, fanged and electrified demon, drive straight for his mark—the weapon wrist. Good old commando stuff. Bacca whirled, and his revolver spat a couple of shots as the dog came in, then fell to the floor as teeth closed on bone. A moment later the fellow's voice rose in a weird choking cry from the floor as Choirboy stood over him, white fangs snicking but a few inches from his throat.

Turner, unwilling to risk a shot because of the close tangle of his accomplice and the dog, came to Bacca's aid. He vaulted the counter again and came in at Choirboy, gun at point. As he passed me, I saw my chance and took it a second before he fired. I did it because of Choirboy, not because of any money in the Citizens' Bank. I landed on Turner's shoulders in a sort of flying tackle and we went down, twisting, flailing and cursing. In a minute I got the hold I wanted; my arms slipped under his from behind, I got a handful of his thick black hair, and jerked his head back hard in a grip shown me by a wrestler I'd written up in the *Banner*. There was a sharp click and that was all.

Later Ed and I and another man had to haul Choirboy off of Juan Bacca and plead with him to give up a battle won, for his own blood was flowing all over the place. Bacca had gotten him with his first shot; but he was challenging still and worrying the downed man with sounds like a circular saw biting through tough green timber.

By that time half a dozen men were piling all over Turner and Bacca and wrapping them up for cold storage, and Bert Taylor, our police chief, had arrived on the scene with a wailing of sirens. But I wasn't paying much attention to all this, for Choirboy had suddenly collapsed in a heap. That bullet had lodged in his lungs. He died a few minutes later with his head in my hands. Ed Hunnicutt never forgave himself for having given the order that sent Choirboy to his death. He went as soft as they make them and so did I, as the two of us carried him out to the police car.

Turner and Bacca, it turned out, were experienced operators, who had worked together for two years, racking up a long series of successful robberies. They'd planned one last easy job in Baysport before making a break to Mexico. Well, that afternoon I did the news story of my life about the attempted robbery and Choirboy's passing, and it wasn't for Baysport alone; it went out over every wire in the country. I never felt so lonesome in my life and I wrote it, you'd better believe, with more than a hint of dimness in my eyes.

Choirboy had gone out in a blaze of glory that made him the town's pet hero all over again. He had proved at firsthand all we had idealized in him: going in to attack

in the face of gunfire where not a man of us dared move, and saving a fat bundle of our public funds.

And so it was that next day there was a regular military funeral held beside Choirboy's little bier, out at Ed Hunnicutt's place. The idea had been Ed's and the town gladly fell in with it. There was a real ceremony with military honors. Corey Boynton and some of his overseas buddies were there in uniform. Someone had even brought a flag, and the crowd of mourners would have done credit to any war hero the country over. Old Reverend Shippen got up and spoke, and so did our mayor, who read to us Choirboy's impressive war record, just as if he'd been human. It was strange. And lovely.

When silence finally fell and we'd come to that place where there's usually a ruffle of drums and a bugler steps out and sounds taps, sweet and low, for the departed, what do you think happened? Somewhere out in the nearby woods a cock quail called in the stillness—high and wild and ringing, and farther off another one answered. A cock quail called. You say to yourself: So what? Mister, Nature doesn't time herself to the split dramatic second like that for nothing. That was more than a cock quail calling. It was a salute to that other phase of Choirboy's life that Army honors couldn't cover. It was a salute to a hunter.

For me it made everything right as rain. It told me plain as gospel that it wasn't really Choirboy we'd lowered into that three-foot hole; not old Choirboy. He'd gone on to join Jesse Hunnicutt, somewhere out there in the bright fall woods—beyond Ed's cornfield.

Hurry Home, Candy

by Meindert DeJong

IN THE FARMHOUSE three miles down the road from the captain's house, the old woman was standing before the big picture window again. The children had suddenly come into sight over a hill. She saw that her husband was with them. "Of course," she said aloud. "How he spoils them." She heard the children's voices, dim, distant, but clear. First the girl's voice: "Candy, Candy, Candy." Then the boy, like an echo: "Candy, Candy!"

The old man trudged at a little distance behind the children. The three seemed to be gradually maneuvering back toward the house. Now they disappeared for a while into the maple wood lot. The children must be getting tired, or they'd given up hope, for as they left the wood lot they came straight across the field toward the house. The old man still followed the fence at the edge of the wood lot.

Suddenly the woman at the picture window started. She was almost sure that for a moment she'd caught a brief movement at the edge of the wood lot, far behind her husband. Now it was gone, swallowed up in the shadows.

The old woman waited. The children had stopped calling, were plodding stolidly on. But there, there—yes, there it was again along the fence row of the field in which the children were walking. The dog must be following the children along the fence row. But now her husband yelled something, and started across to the children. In the moment of the man's yell there was a brief flash, and the dog was gone.

"Oh, he spoiled it. He spoiled it," she disappointedly told herself. "If only he hadn't been there! The little dog was coming to the children."

She hurried across the room to the telephone, gave the operator Captain Carlson's number. . . . "I saw him," she told the captain without any preliminaries. "I just saw him! One brief glimpse. He was following the children at a distance. But then he heard or saw my husband. If my husband hadn't been there, he might have followed the children. But at least now we know that he's alive and around his old haunts, but it looked as if he were hobbling on three legs."

She listened for a few brief moments. "Now, as soon as the children get to the house I'll stuff some sandwiches in their hands and send them right out again. They've been out there since dawn, but I know the moment they hear I saw him they won't be able to rest. And this time I'll keep my husband home. . . . Yes, I'll keep you informed." She hung up and hurried back to the window.

Now the fields were quiet, empty of callings and movements. There were no more footsteps, no more cracklings of twigs and crunchings of old dead leaves. All morning the little dog had listened to the children's voices coming, going, now near, now far, then coming back again. Always calling: "Candy, Candy, Candy." In the girl's high thin voice, "Candy, Candy." In the boy's still higher, shriller voice.

He hadn't stirred from his painful, stiff position under the cordwood pile. But the calling of his name had kept tugging at his memory—a faint, far remembrance of young voices he had once loved.

Silently, eyes staring down the tunnel-like opening under the wood, he had followed the movements of the children as they neared the woodpile. For a flash of a moment he had seen them as they blundered along on the dry twigs on the wood lot floor. But they left the wood lot. Suddenly the boy shrilled out in a last hard call: "Candy, Candy." There was no urging in his voice now, just tired hopelessness. The girl did not add her call. There it remained, that last call.

Suddenly an urge rose in the little dog; he pulled himself stiffly from under the woodpile and stole to the edge of the wood lot. But by the time he had hobbled across the wood lot the children were away in the field. Silently the dog stole along the edge of the field by way of the fence row. He stood staring after the children, screened from them by a bush. At that moment the old man yelled across the field and walked over to the children. The dog turned away. A twig he stepped on jumped up and hit his wounded leg. He cut off one tiny whimper and hobbled back. He crawled under the woodpile again, and lay there in pain. He still heard the going-away sound of the three in the field, but he shut himself away into his loneliness. He stared straight ahead, and every few minutes he swallowed.

The children came into the house in silent defeat. All their fine hopes of the morning were dashed—all their hopes for the bicycles. The grandfather seemed as disappointed and thwarted as the children. The boy threw himself heavily into a chair, surly with defeat, blank-faced because he was so near to tears. "He didn't come," he managed to tell his grandmother.

"I guess he's forgotten us," the girl said bitterly.

The old man said nothing.

"We ate our lunch, but we're still hungry," George told his grandmother. He looked hungrily at the sandwiches on the table.

"I guess he's forgotten us," the girl said again. "We never saw anything of him." She was too sullen with disappointment to be interested in the food.

"No, but I saw him!" their grandmother said. "I saw him, and he started to follow you, and if it hadn't been for your grandfather yelling at you at that moment, he might have come. But the moment he saw a man he disappeared."

"Where, Grandma? Did you really see him? Where?"

"Coming out of our wood lot. So now you grab some sandwiches, and you two get right back there, and this time without your grandfather. But don't hunt around that wood lot, don't go poking and searching for him— just play! Play some of the games you played when he was a puppy. Talk to each other and mention his name a lot, but don't go crashing around looking for him. Then if he still doesn't come, walk away from the wood lot every now and then as if you were starting for home. I'll be watching to see if he comes out again. Do you think you can do that?"

The children nodded solemnly, awed by all their grandmother seemed to know about the little dog. Then George grabbed a handful of sandwiches. "Come on, Catherine, let's go!"

After the children were gone the old woman went to the telephone to make her latest report. The captain listened carefully, and then he told her: "Now that I know where he is, and that he's alive—you understand the children are going to get bicycles for all they've done. And it certainly sounds to me that you've figured it out the best way—having the children play around him as in the old days. You must love and understand dogs."

She snorted. "I'm the old woman that would rather have a picture window than a dog!" she said sharply.

From her post at the picture window the old woman watched the children. It didn't work—her strategy. The children were following her instructions literally. She could see them at times running and playing around the wood lot, then they would make brief marches across the empty field again, but always they kept looking back over their shoulders, and always they hurried back to the wood lot. Maybe they're overdoing it, she thought to herself. They're trying too hard and making it artificial. Maybe they should do what they did this morning—just keep calling his name. She turned as if she had half a mind to go out to them, but then she turned back to the window. "I've a notion," she muttered to herself, "that he's still more afraid of women than of men—she with her broom for a puppy!"

Late in the afternoon the exhausted, disappointed children gave up. They could not manufacture any more play. There was no laughter in them; they were too close to tears. Once more as they trudged away across the field toward the house, the boy sent out his last call: "Candy, Candy." Then they walked on. They did not look back. They'd given up.

"Something went badly wrong," the old woman at the window muttered as she watched the children. "I guessed wrong." Suddenly her eyes flicked back to the wood lot— a slight movement there had caught her eye. There he stood! On a little knoll outside the wood lot, for the first time in plain sight. He had one leg drawn up. He stood staring mutely after the children.

"Call now, call now," the woman at the window urged under her breath. The children trudged on. Still the dog stood there. Suddenly he turned his head. The woman turned her eyes to look where the dog was looking. When she looked back the little dog had disappeared; something in the wood lot must have scared him. "That did it," the woman bitterly told herself. The children came into the house.

The girl and boy walked into the room and stood before their grandmother in utter desolation. "He didn't come," George managed to say. "He's gone, I guess."

"No," their grandmother said. "He isn't. I saw him again just before you came into the house, so he's there.

. . . But don't worry, you've done enough. I suspect he
didn't intend to follow you anyway, just watch you out
of sight. But you two can start right now being happy
again. I talked to Captain Carlson on the phone. And do
you know what he told me? You're each to get a brand-
new bicycle for all you've done!"

They couldn't believe her. It was too sudden a fullness
in the emptiness of their disappointment and defeat.
Their grandmother carefully had to repeat every word
the captain had said.

The girl had a momentary conscience-stricken scare at
the thought of going to the strange man for the reward
when they didn't have the little dog. "Maybe if we do it
once more—just walk from the wood lot across the field to
the house. . . ."

"No," her grandmother decided. "No, you're overtired
and you've done enough. And maybe it isn't even good—
him moving about so much with that bad leg. No, you go
right upstairs now and lie down and rest, and talk about
bicycles until your father comes to take you home." She
smiled at them fondly.

When the children had gone upstairs the old woman
once more went to the telephone, but this time to warn
the captain that the children were coming for their reward. "I seemed to have to do it that way, they were so
beaten and they'd worked so hard all day," she apolo-
gized. She explained that the little dog had briefly
emerged from the wood lot once more. "But I'm afraid he
has no feeling of belonging to them any more. I guess he
belongs wholly to you now. So there's only one thing left
—food! So this is my plan. Tonight I'm once more setting

out my food pan, but tonight I'm going to be cruel and mean about it. The pan's just going to smell of food—oh, maybe a dribble in it to sharpen and tease his hunger. But I suspect that's how he lived the past year—scrounging food from house to house. So if he gets nothing here, he might keep going on to the next house, he might even go so far as your house—and then if you'd have some good food set out. . . ."

The captain eagerly explained that he had already arranged for a big pan of hamburg to be set at his kitchen door.

"Ah," she said, "between the two of us—a little brains and a lot of love. . . . But I'm sorry about the children coming and my just arranging it like that for you, but they were so beaten."

"It's fine about the children, and you are wonderful," he said.

The children had come and gone. Abashed and excited, standing before the captain lying on the couch, they'd been only too eager to be away. They had gone off with their father, dancing with excitement all around him, both talking excitedly to him at the same time. "Two bicycles cost much more than fifty dollars, don't they, Dad?" George had demanded. "But we're just to go to the store and pick them out, and we didn't even find Candy. He's rich, isn't he, Dad?"

"Mine's going to be all red," Catherine had announced. "Bright red, with just a tiny thin white line. . . ."

"Mine's going to be a racer." George had tried to outdo his sister.

"We'll see, we'll see," the distracted father had kept saying over and over.

In the house, Martha, the cleaning woman, was making preparations to leave for the night. "Did you set out the hamburg?" the captain shouted after her.

She answered from the kitchen door. "It's all set, just as you wanted it, and I'm leaving the door open. I'll try to be back about ten in the morning."

That was the last sound until night came after an endless twilight. The window at the couch was open. The crutches were set where the man could reach them. Evening insect sounds shrilled outside the window, but then all sounds slowly drifted into night stillness. The hours wore on. Now, slowly as the hours had gone, it was deep night, and still the man on the couch kept vigil. The phone at his elbow, after a short preliminary ping, shrilled through the silent house.

It was the old woman. "He's been here, and he's gone —three footprints in the smooth wet dirt around my food pan. Now we can only hope he's on his way to you."

"Goodness, have you stayed up all this time?"

"I had to see it through, but now I'm really going to bed. You'll let me know the first thing in the morning, won't you?"

The night was edging toward morning and now the moon was out. The little dog sat on a knoll under an apple tree, the highest point in a high field. He sat tense. He could not see it, but the teasing, luring, lovely odors of

meat came to him again in the field, carried to him on a small night breeze. Across the field rose the tall white house among the pine trees. The food odors came from that house, the house that had been his house.

Now the moon drifted from behind clouds; moonlight glinted along the blue roof against the stark green of the pine trees. It glinted momentarily on the yellow straw broom still hanging in the pine tree. It was as if it gave him courage, the silly, helpless broom hanging there so high. He stole from under the night shadows of the apple tree; he edged a little closer to the house, but then he sat down.

An hour later he had edged into the yard. He carefully kept to the shadows of the outbuildings. At last he neared the garage, the last shadowed building between him and the pan with food in the bare, moonlit yard. He tensed, ready for the last three-legged hobble across the yard, and the snatching of the first hungry mouthful of food. But as he came around the corner of the garage, there in full view stood a broom! A broom stood against the house directly behind the pan of food. The desperation of his hunger oozed out of him. He backed away into the shadows and hobbled away.

Under the apple tree in the high field he stopped to rest. His tortured body, after his long journey, could take no more. He trembled with weakness. He was weak with a terrible hunger, and across the field the food odors came lilting again on the night breezes, and the broom swayed in the pine tree. Suddenly the little dog lifted his head. Out of his tight throat broke the hopeless singsong of his misery. And into it he sang all his helplessness and hopelessness and loneliness and all the misery of brooms and hunger and desertion, and the cruelty of men.

In the house the big man lifted his head, propped himself up. He lay listening to the little dog's wail, as if by the very intensity of his listening he could force the little dog to come closer. But the miserable thin howl came no closer.

"He doesn't dare; he wants to come but doesn't dare," the man said softly.

He lunged up from his couch, grabbed the crutches. His big body wasn't used to them. He made several clumsy tries, but at last he had the crutches under him. He swung himself awkwardly out to the kitchen and the wide-open kitchen door. He stood in the moonlit doorway, peering everywhere. In the field under the apple tree the dog had fallen silent at the first sight of him.

The man on the crutches waited. Then he tentatively tried it. "Candy," he called. "Candy, Candy, Candy."

He listened after each call, but the night lay silent. "Maybe," he muttered to himself, "if I go inside and leave it to the hamburg." He turned. And then he saw the broom the cleaning woman had left standing against the house. Suddenly he was in a towering rage. "That woman!" He muttered savage, violent things; he swung himself toward the broom and grabbed it. Somehow he balanced himself on one crutch and with fierce, wrathful strength swung the broom far from him. It twisted and spiraled, and spun away into a tree. There it clung. The man muttered things at it and violently swung himself into the house, but behind him he left the door wide open.

In the high field under the shadows of the apple tree the little dog had seen it all. Had seen the big man suddenly appear on crutches. Had listened to the big man calling him for the first time by his name. He had listened and he had tested it, but he had not dared to yield to it and obey. He had not dared to believe it. But then he had seen the man lunge at the broom and hurl it twisting through the air. The broom still hung there in the tree, but now it was all over; the great, good man was gone. But the food stood there, and the door stood open.

The little dog came forward a few tentative steps. He sat again. But as he sat an impelling urge came to him to wave his tail, and he got up again. Once more he advanced across the field. Once more he approached the house, but he seemed to have to approach it by the same old hidden cautious way he had approached it before. At last he sat in the shadows of the outbuildings again. He was gathering his last courage. But as he sat in the shadows there came a stomping in the house, and then the captain, awkwardly balancing himself on one crutch, appeared in the doorway once more.

The big man carried a pan, and from the pan came new warm meat odors. Lovely, heavenly warm odors came lilting across the yard. Still the dog sat secret and unseen in the shadows. Now the captain set down the pan with the new warm food in the kitchen, a foot or two beyond the open door. Then the man straightened up, and then came his order clearly across the silent yard. "Candy! Hurry home, Candy. Candy, you come home!" And then with clumsy stompings the man disappeared in the house.

The warm food stood in the kitchen just beyond the

moonlit door. The food stood there, the order of the great good man still stood there: "Hurry home, Candy. Candy, you come home!"

The little dog left the shadows. But he couldn't go straight. He still warily had to circle the buildings on his slow three legs. But every circle brought him closer to the open kitchen door. And now between him and the open door lay only the naked, moonlit yard. And the broom hung in the pine trees.

In the shadows of the garage the little dog sat fighting his last timid hesitation, sat fighting with the compelling odors of the good, warm food, sat testing the last spoken order of the great good man. "Hurry home, Candy. Candy, you come home!" Once more the urge came to him to wag and wave his tail.

The little dog stood up; the little dog had started to obey. And in a moment he would walk across the open yard and through an open door. And then he would be in. Then he would not merely have a pan of food, he'd have a home, he'd have a name, he'd have a love for a great, good man. A love for a man that would grow and grow in a great, good life with the man. A love so huge, and so complete and so eternal, the little dog would hardly be able to encompass it in his one little timid heart.

Hurry home, Candy. Oh, little dog, why don't you go now? Why don't you hurry home?

The little dog stepped out of the shadows, and on three legs the little dog went home.

A Dog Like Pierre

by Ethel McCall Head

AS HE CAME OUT of the American Embassy dining room,
the rain started again. That was one of the bad things
about Paris. It rained all the time. His mother had suggested he eat at the hotel, but they had hamburgers at
the Embassy and it was only a block away.

At the corner he stopped to watch the cars streaming
into the Place de la Concorde. Seven o'clock was the rush
hour. Everyone was going home to dinner but most people didn't live in houses, only apartments. Maybe this
time his parents would be lucky enough to find a real
house with a back yard. Then he could have a dog.

Pulling up the collar of his raincoat, he walked slowly
to the hotel. He took the elevator to the fifth floor, and
Martin invited him to ride up and down for a while after
Terry's parents went out. He liked Martin, who told him
how he wanted to go to New York and work in the Waldorf, where his cousin was a waiter.

Though Terry had never been in the Waldorf, Martin

was sure that Monsieur Terree must have met his cousin —tall he was with a black mustache, and such money he made while he, Martin, was shut up day and night in that cage of an elevator. Sometimes, if there were no passengers, Martin would let Terry run the elevator and then they would talk about the dog Terry was going to get— a dog just like Pierre's!

As Terry entered the room, he could see that his parents and their friends were about to go to dinner. Terry had to listen to Colonel Gilman, who had it all planned that when Terry was grown up, he was to go to West Point. There was no use explaining that instead he wanted to live in California near his grandmother's house and raise dogs.

Just as everyone was about to go, Major Peters beckoned to Terry and led him into his little bedroom. "I've got news for you, boy. Your father's told me you want a dog more than anything in the world. You know we're being sent to Japan, and we're going to give you Fifi."

Terry couldn't answer. He didn't look at the major, but stared at the big purple roses on the wallpaper.

"You know how smart Fifi is. She's got a pedigree a mile long, too."

Someone called from the other room, "Come along, Peters. It's getting late."

He went out as Terry's mother came in to kiss him good night, made him promise to go to bed early. "Isn't it wonderful of the Peters to give us Fifi? I've always loved French poodles. Well, I'll see you in the morning, Terry."

They were gone. Fifi! That silly clipped miniature

poodle. She wasn't a dog at all. Last Sunday at the Peters, all the women had drooled over that stinking Fifi. Mrs. Peters said, *"dansez"* and the dog circled on her hind legs just like a ballet dancer, then sat at a table and ate tea cakes.

Fifi was a sissy dog that he hated. Not like Pierre's dog, Col, a brown-and-white mutt twice as smart as Fifi. That Col could flush a covey of quail. He could retrieve. He could carry a newspaper home. That was the kind of dog he wanted!

When they'd left Rouen, Terry told Pierre that when he got his dog he was going to name him Col, too, and Pierre was real pleased. It was a funny name for a dog because in French, Col meant collar, but Pierre's dog was called that because he had a rough bunch of hair that stuck up from his neck just like a collar. He didn't look anything like Fifi.

And none of the kids in the San Fernando Valley near his grandmother's house had French poodles. They had Cockers that were part Scotty, or shaggy Collies with Boxer noses. Joe had told him that they were really Heinz dogs because they were fifty-seven varieties. But they were good dogs and loved the kids more than the grown-ups. Just the opposite of Fifi. Maybe his mother could have Fifi and he could still get Col. Anyhow, the first thing in the morning he'd talk to his father and tell him he didn't want Fifi.

To get his mind off the poodle, Terry decided to work with the ship model his father had given him for his birthday. It was a funny birthday on board the *Liberté*. There'd been a big cake with his name written on it in red and blue frosting. There'd been spun-sugar roses, but no candles. It was too French. It wasn't like an American birthday party.

Everything was better at home. He wished he could live all the time in the United States. He'd been to Switzerland and England, to Italy and Spain, but he'd never seen Niagara Falls or gone to a Boy Scout camp or a cookout like the kids who lived near his grandmother. Why, he'd never even heard of Wyatt Earp until this last trip back.

He put the model away. Though he tried to keep promises and it was nine o'clock, he didn't feel sleepy and he was sure he'd have nightmares about Fifi. A woman's dog, not what he wanted at all. Opening the window, he leaned on the sill and felt the damp air on his face. It was still raining. Down the street he could hear the voices of the workmen finishing the Café Americain. Putting his head down on his crossed arms, he felt as if he could cry.

When Terry woke the next morning, his father was gone. It was a bad break not to discuss Fifi with him, because his father was pretty understanding, so Terry decided to explain it to his mother.

Dipping his croissant in his chocolate, he said, "I think Fifi is the dumbest dog I ever saw."

"That's silly. You know perfectly well she's exceptionally smart, really a show dog."

If only he could have talked to his father. They were leaving in the morning. There wasn't much time. "I don't see why I can't have the kind of dog I want and not get a darned poodle wished on me just because the Peters can't take her to Japan."

"It was kind of the Peters. Fifi is to be your dog, not mine, though I think she's darling."

"You would, Mother, she's a girl's dog. I want one that'll love me."

"I've never seen a dog that didn't take to you. I'm sure you'll get to like Fifi. Look, the rain has stopped. There's even sunshine."

He looked out at the pale, cold sunshine. Not like it was in California. Maybe, his father could explain to the Peters that they couldn't take Fifi because first they'd have to find a house where the landlord would permit a dog. That would be a real good excuse.

His mother looked up from the morning paper. "Dad won't be home until late. We'll have dinner alone."

Terry put down his croissant. He'd choke if he took another bite. They were stuck with Fifi. He felt as if someone had died. It was Col! Black and white, brown and yellow, the color didn't matter, but the Heinz dog he already loved was dead, as dead as if it had been poisoned or run over. And he felt the same grief!

The next morning, the car loaded, they started up the Champs-Elysées. It was a sunny autumn day, but Terry, wedged in the back seat next to the suitcase, felt no excitement as he usually did when they started off to a new place. Instead, he felt as if he had a lump of ice deep down inside.

When his father stopped in front of the Peters' apartment, Terry felt close to tears, so he concentrated on watching an old man sweep up the leaves of the plane trees with a broom made of twigs.

Then his father, the Peters and Fifi were on the curb.

Major Peters opened the back door, "Here you are, Terry. Take good care of Fifi." He turned to the dog, "O.K., girl, get in. Terry's your new master."

But Fifi stood firmly on the pavement and, finally, Major Peters had to pick her up and put her in the seat next to Terry. He said to himself, "So you don't like me. That's just dandy, because I don't like you either."

Then he noticed his father standing there with that nice smile he had and he knew he couldn't let his father down. He didn't know how Terry felt about that dog.

"Thank you, Mrs. Peters, and you, sir. It was very kind of you to give me Fifi." He echoed his mother's words.

Mrs. Peters gave Fifi a last pat. "She's your dog, Terry, just give her a little time and she'll be crazy about you and you'll love her as much as we do."

To himself he thought, "That's what you think!"

As they started off, Fifi sat quietly by the window. Terry noticed she'd been freshly clipped, looked as if she'd just had a permanent, all curly, like his mother when she'd come home from the beauty shop. For a dog it was terrible, and she wore a wide red collar with brass studs.

After lunch in Chartres, where they'd left Fifi in the car, they went to the cathedral because Terry's father had always wanted to get a color shot of the Rose Window when there was sunshine. Terry thought the cathedral was too big, not as nice as the little church in San Fernando, so he sat in the car with Fifi.

Putting her head down on the suitcase, she stared at him as if she were deciding whether she liked him or not. It made him jittery, so taking her leash off, he let her out, thinking she might run away, try to get back to the Peters.

That's what Pierre's dog would do, but she came right back and when they started off again, she put her head in his lap.

He pushed her into the corner, where she curled up and went to sleep. Later in the afternoon, when they stopped for gas, his mother suggested that Fifi sit up in front for a while. She patted and cooed to her the way women do with dogs, but Fifi whined and as soon as his mother let go, she jumped into the back seat next to him.

His father was pleased. "That's amazing, son, she already seems to prefer you."

"She's just more comfortable back here."

That night at the hotel in Tours, they took in a basket which Mrs. Peters had given them, saying Fifi loved it, but the next morning when Terry woke up, the dog was on the end of his bed. He gave her a little kick and she jumped off right away, as if her feelings were hurt, and went to her basket. It seemed sort of mean, but he wasn't going to have that lousy dog on his bed. She seemed to understand that he wanted no part of her, but still wouldn't pay any attention to his parents.

The next night, when his mother fixed Fifi's food in the bathroom, the dog wouldn't touch it. His father said, "You try to get her to eat, Terry."

He knelt on the floor, rubbed her ears and said, "It's good, Fifi, good supper." She looked straight at him, her little sharp nose turned up, and then started to eat. When she finished, she picked up the rubber dish in her mouth, dropped it in the bidet and barked.

From her room, his mother called, "What's the matter with her?"

Terry said, "Don't ask me. The dummy just stands here by the bidet and keeps barking."

His parents came to the bathroom door. "Maybe she wants a drink, turn the water on."

But when Terry turned the water on, Fifi didn't drink. She just walked away and got into her basket.

"That's the cutest thing I ever saw," said Terry's mother. "She's been trained to drop her dirty dish in the bidet where it can be washed."

Terry said, "Well, at least it makes more sense than dancing on her hind legs."

On the way down to Toulouse, Terry figured out how he could have Col, too. His father had said he'd be too busy to look at houses and that Terry, because he spoke French so well, would have to go with his mother to interpret. Terry was sure that if a landlord would let them have one dog, it was possible to manage another one. His grandmother had given him a check for his birthday and he had some of his allowance saved up. He'd give the real-estate agent a good fat tip. Ten dollars was quite a lot.

The first morning in Toulouse, his father said, "Now, Terry, you carry on for Mother. We shouldn't pay more than eighty-five dollars a month, but the first condition of renting is that we can have Fifi. Mother and I can't get over how she's adopted you."

"I don't mean a thing to her. She's lonesome."

"Well, she acts as if she hated me. Don't ask me why," said his mother.

"She'll get over that." And he thought to himself, "I'll say she will when I get Col."

After lunch, the real-estate man came to the hotel and they started out. He spoke no English. Fifi went, too. Terry's mother said, "Let's face it. The French are mad about poodles. It's the one kind of dog they wouldn't object to."

But it turned out that for the first time since they'd gotten her, Fifi was a nuisance. She went into each house with them, sniffed around, crawled under the beds and then went to the front door and whined to get out. Terry's mother said, "She thinks they're awful and so do I."

Certainly, Fifi didn't like any of the houses and none of them had back yards. At the fourth house the dog made such a fuss that his mother said crossly, "For heaven's sake, Terry, take her out. I can't concentrate with her whining."

Terry and Fifi stood waiting on the sidewalk when a woman and a little boy came by. The woman reached down to pat Fifi, who backed up, but when the boy patted her, she wagged her tail, licked his hand and acted friendly.

Terry was surprised. He couldn't believe it, but maybe Fifi did like kids better than grownups. His mother came out discouraged.

The *marchand de biens*, who realized they didn't like any of the houses, said to Terry, "Please explain to Madame that there is one small villa which is a jewel, so perfect it is. And for only a very little more than the price your father wishes to pay."

Terry said, "Let's see it, monsieur. The price, perhaps, can be arranged."

The house looked nice. It was on a quiet street, lined

with trees, and right in front was a small park. Terry thought it would be a swell place for the dogs to play! The house was white with blue shutters; the gravelled terrace, enclosed by a low fence, was bordered by flowers. Terry's mother liked it right away, but as they got out of the car, she said, "Leave Fifi locked in. She's been a nuisance."

Inside, the house wasn't as cold as the others. Sunshine poured in from the south windows. Terry thought the salon was real nice with a real fireplace where you could toast marshmallows. When they reached the kitchen, the real-estate man was smiling as if he had a big surprise for them.

"Regardez, Madame. C'est merveilleuse, n'est-ce pas?" He explained that at a frightful expense, but truly, the owner had made a real American kitchen.

Terry's mother couldn't believe it. "Look, linoleum drainboards, good cupboards and an electric refrigerator. Terry, ask him how much it is and if we can have Fifi. It's out of this world."

Terry turned to the man, whose waxed mustache seemed trembling with excitement. The rent was ninety-five a month. The man explained there was service for twelve, the blankets and linens of the best quality, even a gas furnace. It was really too cheap, *bien sur,* and only a little more than the houses which Madame had not liked at all.

Terry was sure his father wouldn't object to ten bucks a month more. "And dogs, Monsieur Lernet, are they permitted?"

"You mean the beautiful Fifi? A true French dog. A

lady. Yes, that I am sure can be arranged with the proprietor. Such a dog he has himself."

"Not one dog, monsieur, but two. Fifi is the dog of my mother. I shall have another. For your trouble in arranging this, I'll give you three thousand francs." Terry tried to sound like his father.

But the *marchand* got real mad. He started talking fast as if Terry had insulted him. He threw up his hands, shrugged his shoulders. One dog, no question about that, but two dogs! *Non, non, non!* Many owners permitted no dogs. They were destructive; they made messes. It is asking too much, altogether too much to demand two dogs in a furnished house.

"*Merci bien, monsieur*. In that case, we won't consider this house."

While the agent looked up, Terry's mother said, "He was awfully cross. He said we couldn't have Fifi, didn't he?"

"That's right."

"How stupid that they won't let us have that well-trained little dog! It's the only house I want." Standing outside on the terrace in front of the pretty villa, Terry thought his mother looked as if she were ready to cry.

"There's only one more house on the list. Then, it's just apartments."

"Well, I'm pooped, but we better see it."

It was almost twilight when they reached the last house. It was an ugly brown with the paint peeling off the shutters. Inside, it was damp, as if no one had lived in it for a long time. Terry's mother complained about the kitchen. It was a dark, musty little hole, she said.

The agent explained to Terry that here he was sure that they could have two dogs, because the widow who owned the house was in great need of renting it at once. No doubt, it could be arranged if *les Americains* put down a good cushion to cover any damage the dogs might cause.

Fifi was barking at the front door. She hated this house most of all, but Terry was happy. He'd managed it—a house where they could have two dogs. Fifi and Col! He turned to his mother and said excitedly, "They'll let us have Fifi here."

"I don't know what to say. It's better than the first ones we saw, but it hasn't any of the charm of that darling one by the park with that wonderful kitchen."

"But this one's only eighty a month and that's even less money than Dad said we should pay."

"It's so gloomy. Even Fifi didn't like it."

Terry felt ashamed. His mother sounded so sad. Somehow, he didn't feel so happy now, so he said, "There's no rush. We can decide tomorrow after we talk it over with Dad."

That night Terry's mother had his dinner sent up to the room because she and his father were going out. Terry fed Fifi first; she licked his hand and seemed awfully glad to be back in the hotel. When his father came in, he looked tired.

"Any luck?"

Terry cut his veal into little pieces. He wasn't hungry. He listened to his mother tell how terrible all the houses were, except for the one by the park, and there, no Fifi.

She said the brown one wasn't bad and a dog was O.K., but the kitchen was impossible and even with Terry wanting a dog so much, it was something to ask her to cope with that dark hole.

Then Terry's father got cross. "A promise is a promise. If French women can produce such wonderful food in bad kitchens, why can't you? No wonder they say American women are spoiled."

Terry left his dinner almost untouched and went to his room. He didn't like to hear his parents quarrel; usually they were so happy. When he went to bed, Fifi settled herself on the pillow next to him. He was so worried that he didn't push her away. He'd told his mother a whopping lie, the first really big one in his whole life. She could have the house she wanted with Fifi. The poodle seemed to know he was upset. He rubbed her ears. "If it weren't for you, dummy, everything would be all right. I could just have Col."

Fifi tipped her head to one side. In the dim light, she looked sort of wise and kindly like his grandmother. What a silly thing to think! Fifi lay down again, but every now and then she licked him. Terry knew she was trying to comfort him. He didn't sleep well. He had nightmares in which Fifi looked at him with her big eyes as if she knew he'd been a dirty little sneak.

The next morning, his father said, "Terry, Mother was disappointed last night about the good house where we can't have Fifi, so this morning you go and look again at the brown house. It sounds like our best best."

Terry watched his mother pour some coffee. "Maybe

I could slipcover the shabby furniture. I hate to give up that adorable house, but so what? If the landlord would let you paint the kitchen white, it would help, Jim."

It's funny, Terry thought, how you don't see your own mother, not really, except when she's so nice, except when you realize she'll give up something awfully important to her, for you.

When they got in the car with the agent, Terry said, "Mother, I told him we'd just look once more at the white house, the one with the swell kitchen."

"Why, if we can't have Fifi there?"

"Maybe I could talk him into it." He blushed, knowing Fifi was welcome there, a real French dog—only not two dogs!

When they reached the villa, Fifi went in with them this time. She sniffed around as she had done in the other houses, but she didn't go to the front door and didn't fuss at all. As his mother admired the electric refrigerator, Terry and the poodle went into the salon. Bright sunshine splashed over the pink furniture. Toulouse was nicer than Paris. It hadn't rained at all. Toulouse was almost as nice as California.

He let Fifi out and stood on the doorstep. In the park some little kids were rolling their hoops, their mothers sitting on benches knitting. A boy on his bicycle, the basket filled with crusty loaves of French bread, went by and waved to Terry, who waved back.

Terry looked after the French boy. It certainly would be good to have a friend who lived near and had a bicycle.

Fifi stretched out on the gravel in the warm sunshine,

perfectly happy. Terry had an idea. Softly, but still as a command, he called, "Here, Col. . . ."

She sat up, tipping her head as she listened. Then, she came running to him. He scratched her ears. "Good Col. You like it here, don't you?"

She put up her paw to shake hands. It sort of scared him that she'd come so fast when he called her. How can a dog be that smart?

Going back into the house, Terry knew what he had to do. "Monsieur Lernet, are you sure we can't have two dogs here? As I said yesterday, I'll give you three thousand francs if you can arrange it." Again he tried to sound like his father.

The real-estate agent got excited, started telling Terry again that it was not possible at all; that only last night in checking, the owner had said one dog and at the brown house, two dogs. Why was it so difficult to comprehend?

Terry smiled. "O.K., we'll take this house. Let's go back to the hotel so my father can sign the papers."

Monsieur Lernet said firmly, "Not two dogs? Only the French poodle."

"Just Fifi, monsieur."

Terry turned to his mother. He had never felt so good in his whole life. "We're renting this house. We can have Fifi."

"You're wonderful, Terry, but how you finagled it I'll never know."

He grinned. That would come later.

"Where's Fifi? She's been so nervous everywhere."

"Not here. She's asleep on the terrace."

When they were outside Terry called, hoping it would work again, "Here, Col."

His mother said, "You mean Fifi . . ."

The dog jumped up, walked over to Terry and sat down on the doorstep next to him.

"No, not Fifi. She already knows I've changed her name to Col."

The poodle rubbed herself against Terry's leg. She looked as if she were smiling. Nuts to those Heinz dogs, Terry thought. Col was practically human.

The Sheep and the Dog

by Aesop

IN THE DAYS when animals could speak, some sheep said to their master:

"We do not understand how it is that you give us only grass which we can find easily for ourselves, when you feed the dog upon all the good things that come from your own table. It is not fair, for we make you rich with our lambs and our wool, while the dog gives you nothing in return for all your favor."

Then the dog, who had been listening to this speech, cried out:

"Yes, but you must remember that it is I who prevents you from being stolen by thieves or devoured by wolves. If I were not there to guard you, you would not be able to eat the grass, for fear of being killed."

This answer contented the sheep, and ever since they have agreed that the dog is worthy of all the honor shown him.

Jean Labadie's Big Black Dog

by Natalie Savage Carlson

ONCE IN ANOTHER TIME, Jean Labadie was the most popular storyteller in the parish. He acted out every story so that it would seem real.

When he told about the great falls of Niagara, he made a booming noise deep in his throat and whirled his fists around each other. Then each listener could plainly hear the falls and see the white water churning and splashing as if it were about to pour down on his own head. But Jean Labadie had to stop telling his stories about the *loup-garou,* that demon who takes the shape of a terrible animal and pounces upon those foolish people who go out alone at night. Every time the storyteller dropped down on all fours, rolled his eyes, snorted, and clawed at the floor, his listeners ran away from him in terror.

It was only on the long winter evenings that Jean had time to tell these tales. All the rest of the year, he worked hard with his cows and his pigs and his chickens.

One day Jean Labadie noticed that his flock of chickens was getting smaller and smaller. He began to suspect that his neighbor, André Drouillard, was stealing them. Yet he never could catch André in the act.

For three nights running, Jean took his gun down from the wall and slept in the henhouse with his chickens. But the only thing that happened was that his hens were disturbed by having their feeder roost with them, and they stopped laying well. So Jean sighed and put his gun back and climbed into his bed again.

One afternoon when Jean went to help his neighbor mow the weeds around his barn, he found a bunch of gray chicken feathers near the fence. Now he was sure

that André was taking his chickens, for all of his neighbor's chickens were scrawny white things.

He did not know how to broach the matter to André without making an enemy of him. And when one lives in the country and needs help with many tasks, it is a great mistake to make an enemy of a close neighbor. Jean studied the matter as his scythe went swish, swish through the tall weeds. At last he thought of a way out.

"Have you seen my big black dog, André?" he asked his neighbor.

"What big black dog?" asked André. "I didn't know you had a dog."

"I just got him from the Indians," said Jean. "Someone has been stealing my chickens so I got myself a dog to protect them. He is a very fierce dog, bigger than a wolf and twice as wild."

Jean took one hand off the scythe and pointed to the ridge behind the barn.

"There he goes now," he cried, "with his big red tongue hanging out of his mouth. See him?"

André looked but could see nothing.

"Surely you must see him. He runs along so fast. He lifts one paw this way and another paw that way."

As Jean said this, he dropped the scythe and lifted first one hand in its black glove and then the other.

André looked at the black gloves going up and down like the paws of a big black dog. Then he looked toward the ridge. He grew excited.

"Yes, yes," he cried, "I do see him now. He is running along the fence. He lifts one paw this way and another paw that way, just like you say."

Jean was pleased that he was such a good actor he could make André see a dog that didn't exist at all.

"Now that you have seen him," he said, "you will know him if you should meet. Give him a wide path and don't do anything that will make him suspicious. He is a very fierce watchdog."

André promised to stay a safe distance from the big black dog.

Jean Labadie was proud of himself over the success of his trick. No more chickens disappeared. It seemed that his problem was solved.

Then one day André greeted him with, "I saw your big black dog in the road today. He was running along lifting one paw this way and another paw that way. I got out of his way, you can bet my life!"

Jean Labadie was pleased and annoyed at the same time. Pleased that André believed so completely in the big black dog that he actually could see him. He was also annoyed because the big black dog had been running down the road when he should have been on the farm.

Another day André leaned over the fence.

"Good day, Jean Labadie," he said. "I saw your big black dog on the other side of the village. He was jumping over fences and bushes. Isn't it a bad thing for him to wander so far away? Someone might take him for the *loup-garou.*"

Jean Labadie was disgusted with his neighbor's good imagination.

"André," he asked, "how can my dog be on the other side of the village when he is right here at home? See him walking through the yard, lifting one paw this way and another paw that way?"

André looked in Jean's yard with surprise.

"And so he is," he agreed. "My faith, what a one he is! He must run like lightning to get home so fast. Perhaps you should chain him up. Someone will surely mistake such a fast dog for the *loup-garou.*"

Jean shrugged hopelessly.

"All right," he said. "Perhaps you are right. I will chain him near the henhouse."

"They will be very happy to hear that in the village," said André. "Everyone is afraid of him. I have told them all about him, how big and fierce he is, how his long red tongue hangs out of his mouth and how he lifts one paw this way and another paw that way."

Jean was angry.

"I would thank you to leave my dog alone, André Drouillard," he said stiffly.

"Oh, ho, and that I do!" retorted André. "But today on the road he growled and snapped at me. I would not be here to tell the story if I hadn't taken to a tall maple tree."

Jean Labadie pressed his lips together.

"Then I will chain him up this very moment." He gave a long low whistle. "Come, fellow! Here, fellow!"

André Drouillard took to his heels.

Of course, this should have ended the matter, and Jean Labadie thought that it had. But one day when he went to the village to buy some nails for his roof, he ran into Madame Villeneuve in a great how-does-it-make of excitement.

"Jean Labadie," she cried to him, "you should be

ashamed of yourself, letting that fierce dog run loose in the village."

"But my dog is chained up in the yard at home," said Jean.

"So André Drouillard told me," said Madame, "but he has broken loose. He is running along lifting one paw this way and another paw that way, with the broken chain dragging in the dust. He growled at me and bared his fangs. It's a lucky thing his chain caught on a bush or I would not be talking to you now."

Jean sighed.

"Perhaps I should get rid of my big black dog," he said. "Tomorrow I will take him back to the Indians."

So next day Jean hitched his horse to the cart and waited until he saw André Drouillard at work in his garden. Then he whistled loudly toward the yard, made a great show of helping his dog climb between the wheels and drove past André's house with one arm curved out in a bow, as if it were around the dog's neck.

"*Au revoir*, André!" he called. Then he looked at the empty half of the seat. "Bark good-bye to André Drouillard, fellow, for you are leaving here forever."

Jean drove out to the Indian village and spent the day with his friends, eating and talking. It seemed a bad waste of time when there was so much to be done on the farm, but on the other hand, it was worth idling all day in order to end the big black dog matter.

Dusk was falling as he rounded the curve near his home. He saw the shadowy figure of André Drouillard waiting for him near his gate. A feeling of foreboding came over Jean.

"What is it?" he asked his neighbor. "Do you have some bad news for me?"

"It's about your big black dog," said André. "He has come back home. Indeed he beat you by an hour. It was that long ago I saw him running down the road to your house with his big red tongue hanging out of his mouth and lifting one paw this way and another paw that way."

Jean was filled with rage. For a twist of tobacco, he would have struck André with his horsewhip.

"André Drouillard," he shouted, "you are a liar! I just left the big black dog with the Indians. They have tied him up."

André sneered.

"A liar am I? We shall see who is the liar. Wait until others see your big black dog running around again."

So Jean might as well have accused André of being a chicken thief in the first place, for now they were enemies anyway. And he certainly might as well have stayed at home and fixed his roof.

Things turned out as his neighbor had hinted. Madame Villeneuve saw the big black dog running behind her house. Henri Dupuis saw him running around the corner of the store. Delphine Langlois even saw him running through the graveyard among the tombstones. And always as he ran along, he lifted one paw this way and another paw that way.

There came that day when Jean Labadie left his neighbor chopping wood all by himself, because they were no longer friends, and drove into the village to have his black mare shod. While he was sitting in front of the blacksmith shop, André Drouillard came galloping up at a great speed. He could scarcely hold the reins, for one hand was cut and bleeding.

A crowd quickly gathered.

"What is wrong, André Drouillard?" they asked.

"Have you cut yourself?"

"Where is Dr. Brisson? Someone fetch Dr. Brisson."

André Drouillard pointed his bleeding hand at Jean Labadie.

"His big black dog bit me," he accused. "Without warning, he jumped the fence as soon as Jean drove away and sank his teeth into my hand."

There was a gasp of horror from every throat. Jean Labadie reddened. He walked over to André and stared at the wound.

"It looks like an ax cut to me," he said.

Then everybody grew angry at Jean Labadie and his big black dog. They threatened to drive them both out of the parish.

"My friends," said Jean wearily, "I think it is time for this matter to be ended. The truth of it is that I have no big black dog. I never had a big black dog. It was all a joke."

"Aha!" cried André. "Now he is trying to crawl out of the blame. He says he has no big black dog. Yet I have seen it with my own eyes, running around and lifting one paw this way and another paw that way."

"I have seen it, too," cried Madame Villeneuve. "It ran up and growled at me."

"And I."

"And I."

Jean Labadie bowed his head.

"All right, my friends," he said. "There is nothing more I can do about it. I guess that big black dog will eat me out of house and home for the rest of my life."

"You mean you won't make things right about this hand?" demanded André Drouillard.

"What do you want me to do?" asked Jean.

"I will be laid up for a week at least," said André Drouillard, "and right at harvest time. Then, too, there may be a scar. But for two of your plumpest pullets, I am willing to overlook the matter and be friends again."

"That is fair," cried Henri Dupuis.

"It is just," cried the blacksmith.

"A generous proposal," agreed everyone.

"And now we will return to my farm," said Jean Labadie, "and I will give André two of my pullets. But all of you must come. I want witnesses."

A crowd trooped down the road to watch the transaction. It was almost as large as the one that had attended Tante Odette's skunk party.

After Jean had given his neighbor two of his best pullets, he commanded the crowd, "Wait!"

He went into the house. When he returned, he was carrying his gun.

"I want witnesses," explained Jean, "because I am going to shoot my big black dog. I want everyone to see this happen."

The crowd murmured and surged. Jean gave a long low whistle toward the henhouse.

"Here comes my big black dog." He pointed. "You can seen how he runs to me with his big red tongue hanging out and lifting one paw this way and another paw that way."

Everyone saw the big black dog.

Jean Labadie lifted his gun to his shoulder, pointed it at nothing and pulled the trigger. There was a deafening roar and the gun kicked Jean to the ground. He arose and brushed off his blouse. Madame Villeneuve screamed and Delphine Langlois fainted.

"There," said Jean, brushing away a tear, "it is done. That is the end of my big black dog. Isn't that true?"

And everyone agreed that the dog was gone for good.

So remember this, my friends: If you must make up a big black dog, do not allow others to help or you may find that you are no longer the dog's master.

Wee Joseph

by *William MacKellar*

DAVIE'S EYES popped in his head. A slow pounding came from under his blue wool jersey where his heart was. Again he looked into Mr. Blaikie's face. And again he looked at the squirming little creature that the farmer held in his hands.

"And you want only sixpence for him?" he repeated.

"That's all, Davie Campbell," the farmer said heartily. "And a fine beast he is, too."

Davie felt his breath strangle in his throat. He put out his hands. The farmer placed the little dog between the cupped fingers. For a long moment Davie just stood, too filled with emotion to speak. Gently he eased his forefinger down the little dog's back. It was strange how thin and uneven the fur was. Still, he was only a pup. That would explain it.

"Aye, it's the fine one he is," Mr. Blaikie said. "The fine one indeed." He winked slyly at the boy. "I've been saving him for yourself, Davie Campbell."

The boy nodded but did not answer. He had never

liked Mr. Blaikie very much. As a matter of fact he couldn't recall anyone in the whole village of Stranmore ever having said anything kind about the farmer. Still it was good of him to have saved the little pup just for him. Just went to show how wrong people could be about other people sometimes.

Again Davie's finger trailed across the pup's skimpy coat. It was queer how many colors it had. Most dogs that Davie had seen had only two colors. *This* little pup—why, it was a rainbow of all kinds of hues—white and black and brown and russet and pink! Surely there had never been such a wonderfully colored dog!

"Aye, it's the grand dog he is for certain, Mr. Blaikie," he agreed. "Will you look at the rare markings on him? I'm thinking there will not be many like him in these parts."

Mr. Blaikie laughed as though Davie had just said something very funny. "Aye, he's different, I'll say *that* for him. A rare kind as you rightly said, Davie Campbell."

"And you want only sixpence for him, Mr. Blaikie?"

The farmer nodded. His eyes, too close together, narrowed slightly. His face no longer wore its smile of good humor when he spoke.

"You've got the money?" he snapped. "But of course you have! Or why would you be asking for the wee dog?" He stretched out his big hand and waited.

Davie hesitated. The sixpence in his pocket was a lot of money. It was everything he had—the sum of all his work for the past month. His father would be angry at first when he learned it had been spent. But when he caught sight of the wee dog, he would understand. Holding the pup in one hand, Davie dug his fingers into the pocket of his knee-length trousers. Slowly he withdrew the small silver coin and dropped it into the farmer's hand. Mr. Blaikie's crafty face was all smiles again.

"Mind, you take good care of him!" He chuckled as he turned away. "There will not be many like him in these parts."

Suddenly he laughed again, just as he had laughed before. Davie could see nothing funny in what he had said. Still, if Mr. Blaikie wanted to laugh that was *his* business. Anyway, who cared? For a moment he watched as the farmer turned and walked away. Then his eyes went to the small bundle of uneven fur that lay cradled in his hands. A great joy rose like a hot flame in Davie Campbell. Tenderly he poked his finger under a round pink nose. He was rewarded a moment later when a small red tongue curled out and took a solemn lick at his finger.

"Aye," he said huskily. "It's plain to see you're a grand dog. A grand dog, indeed!"

Again Davie ran his finger admiringly over the pup's body. It was strange, though, how close the ribs seemed to be against the coat. Almost as if there were no flesh at all on the wee body, as if the pup had been starved. But who would starve a fine wee dog like this now? Davie dismissed the thought at once.

"I'll call you Joseph," he said suddenly, and knew that of all names, *this* was the right one. For hadn't they just read last week in Sunday school about Joseph and his coat of many colors?

"Joseph," he said softly. "I'm talking to you, Joseph."

The freckled nose wrinkled. A gangling ear twitched ever so slightly. A moist brown eye winked open.

"He knows his name already," marveled Davie. Pride made the words tight in his throat.

The scent of the bog myrtle rode the soft hill wind and moved with a slow sweetness in Davie's nostrils. Joseph lay crooked in his arms as he started the journey back to his home. Davie's bare feet moved easily through the coarse, dry heather. When first he had doffed his shoes with the coming of the warm June days, the bracken fronds and the spiky heather shoots had seemed harsh against his feet. Now he could take even the thorniest undergrowth in stride. He hummed as he walked.

"Good day to you, Davie," a man called from a small granite house with trim green shutters.

"Good day to you, Mr. Leckie," Davie said to the schoolmaster.

The teacher leaned on the gate leading to his garden and smiled.

"What have you there, Davie?"

Davie smiled back proudly. "A dog, Mr. Leckie. And it's a fine dog he is, too!"

"H-m." Mr. Leckie's lips pursed slightly as he looked at the dog. "Where did you get him, Davie?"

"From Mr. Blaikie." He stopped. He knew there was something else he should say. "For sixpence."

"For sixpence?" A shadow fell across the schoolmaster's face. "May I look at him, Davie?"

Carefully the boy handed the dog over. "His name's Joseph."

"H-m." Again Mr. Leckie's lips set in a tight line. His

long fingers moved slowly over the dog. The shadow darkened on his face.

"You paid sixpence for him, you said?"

"Aye."

"I see." With a grunt the schoolmaster returned the dog to the boy. "I'm afraid our Mr. Blaikie is as big a rascal as people say he is."

Davie stopped, his hands around Joseph. "What do you mean?"

"Just that this Joseph of yours isn't quite the fine dog Mr. Blaikie claimed he was."

Davie stared, then leaped to defend Joseph. "Are you saying he's not got the grand blood at all?"

The schoolmaster let his hand drop gently on Davie's shoulder. "I'm afraid he's just a mongrel, Davie. This dog was evidently one of a large litter. The mother couldn't take care of him. Mr. Blaikie didn't bother. Why just look at the poor thing, Davie! He's skin and bones!"

"But he's only a wee pup," Davie protested. "Besides, why should Mr. Blaikie see that the other pups were fed and not Joseph?"

Mr. Leckie sighed. "Tastes in dogs differ, Davie. Your taste is the right one for you. However, most people wouldn't like Joseph. All his markings are in the wrong places. And he's got the oddest colors I've ever seen. Besides, his legs are too short and his body is too long and his ears don't match. Why, you'd think they had been meant for two different dogs." He shook his head sadly. "I'm afraid, Davie," he said, "most people would call Joseph a misfit."

"A mis . . . ?" Davie clamped his jaws tight to contain

the bitter word. Not Joseph! His blue eyes blazed fiercely as he backed away from the schoolmaster and held Joseph in his arms.

"As you said before, Mr. Leckie, it's a matter of taste. Good day to you." Quickly he turned away.

Mr. Leckie called after him. "Good day to you, too, Davie."

What was the matter with the man, thought Davie angrily. Aye, and him a schoolteacher, too! Calling Joseph a misfit! It was a wonder Joseph hadn't leaped at his throat. Aye, a wonder indeed! He lifted his arms and held his face close to Joseph. He could feel the soft warmth steal up from the pup's body. The coarse hair moved ever so gently against Davie's cheek in time with the scrawny little creature's breathing.

Joseph was fast asleep.

"Now, Ian," Nell Campbell said with a show of brightness, "there's no reason at all to look so surprised. It's just a wee dog that Davie brought home."

"We have no room for dogs here," Ian Campbell said. "Nor food either, I'm thinking." He shrugged off his work jacket and tossed it over a straight-backed chair. He frowned at Joseph, asleep in his box.

"Where did you get this beast, Davie?" he asked calmly.

He did not look angry. Encouraged, Davie told the story of how he had got Joseph from Mr. Blaikie. At first he had meant to hide the fact that he had paid for him. Now, with Joseph's worth at stake, he thought it best to mention the sixpence that the dog cost him.

"Aye, but he's worth it, he is," the boy finished. "For he's a fine dog!" He stopped, knowing there should be something else he should say. "Aye, and it's the great help he'll be around the house."

The silence was thick in the kitchen. It seemed to drip from the very beams in the ceiling. Then it was torn asunder by the sound of his father's voice.

"You paid sixpence for the like of that! Hard-earned money thrown away sinfully to a rogue and a thief like Blaikie! Could you not have seen that the dog is worthless?"

The voice was a terrible loudness in Davie's ears. It was hard to think. There was a queer spinning and tumbling in his mind, and it was impossible to sort the words out. The words that needed to be spoken if Joseph were to stay.

"Have you no tongue?" Ian Campbell said.

"He's not worthless! I don't care what you think!" And now that the words were there, the courage was there, too. He looked with defiance at this man whom he feared and was beginning to hate. "There's the grand blood in him. Mr. Blaikie said so. Aye, and so did old Tam Menzies!"

Little points of light stabbed at the darkness in Ian Campbell's eyes. For a moment his big hand went up and Davie felt a quick weakness in his legs as he waited for the blow to fall. But no blow fell. Davie blinked his eyes open.

"It is well for you, Davie, that I am slow to anger," Ian Campbell said between thin lips. He breathed deeply, and his outgoing breath was a soft rasp in the heavy air. "I am not in the habit of reasoning with my sons. Yet

I would not want you to think I am unjust." He stopped and closed his eyes with a quick tiredness. "I am a very just man, Davie."

"Then be just with Joseph here!" Davie pleaded.

Ian Campbell nodded. His dark face was calm again. The sudden tiredness gone. He pointed to a chair. "Do you see that chair, Davie?"

He nodded. "Aye."

"And what will it be for?"

" To sit on. "

"And those shoes under the bed?"

"To put on your feet."

"And that plate, Davie?"

"To eat from."

Ian Campbell stopped. "They all have a purpose, eh?"

"Aye."

"They all have a use?"

"Aye."

Ian Campbell's long finger stabbed forward and pointed straight at Joseph. "And what of that miserable beast? What purpose—aye, what use is *he?*" His voice cracked like a lash, and Davie flinched.

"He—he—" the boy floundered. He tried hard to think of something to say on Joseph's behalf. Somehow Joseph didn't have any purpose, really. Except to make the world a little brighter by just being in it.

"I'm waiting, Davie."

He looked again at the dog. "I just like him," he said gravely. Somehow there didn't seem to be anything more one could add to that.

"Vain affection!" thundered Ian Campbell. His brow

was black. "This is no useful dog! It's but a cur for preening and sinful pampering! Our bread is hard-earned, Davie Campbell. I will not have it used to feed a useless beast. Do you hear that?"

"Aye," he said. His voice was a small dryness in his throat. He did not look at his father.

"Good," Ian Campbell said grimly. He paused, then said with a quick mildness, "You can keep him here for the night. There will be no harm in it."

Davie did not answer. There was nothing to say. Joseph still slept. What was it his mother had said? *"In many ways he was not a very happy man, that Joseph of yours. I'm thinking your wee dog was too well named."*

His mother was right of course. Joseph hadn't been the happiest of men. With his coat of many colors he had been sold into slavery. He had known hunger. He had known loneliness. He had been in prison. Yet in the end everything had worked out well.

Somehow the thought was a slight comfort to Davie as he took his place at the table.

There was a small canvas bag near Davie's bed when he woke. He did not have to ask who had left it. Or what it was for. He tried not to look at it as he forced down the steaming plate of porridge that his mother gave him. The oatmeal, usually so smooth, seemed coarse against his tongue. Even the cold milk seemed flat and without taste.

When his mother's back was turned, he stole out of the kitchen with Joseph. He sensed that this morning his mother would have kissed him. And had she done so, there was no saying what he might do. Why, he might even break out into tears!

Her back was turned as he started to draw the door closed. He looked at her with eyes swimming with love and hurt. And then just as he stood there with his hand on the knob, Joseph let out a small whinny of impatience. Davie froze. He waited for his mother to swing around and discover him. But she did not turn. Made no sign that she had even heard. But she *must* have heard. It was only as he silently drew the door closed that he understood. His mother had read his heart. Had guessed at the tears behind his eyes. At his need to be alone. It was no accident that her back was turned. No accident that she had not heard Joseph's whimper. And the tears that she did not see were bright in his eyes as he closed the door and slipped away from the cottage.

When Davie had arisen to find his father gone, his last hope to save Joseph had vanished. For how was Joseph to be spared if his father did not give the word? Now all that lay ahead was the bitter trip up the hills to where the Angus River flowed. Only that and a certain task that made his heart sick to think about.

It had rained during the night, but with the morning the skies had cleared. As they passed under the giant sycamore outside, the breeze from the hills sent a gentle spray of moisture down on the boy and the dog. Joseph shook himself and sniffed his annoyance. Little drops of rain dripped down his nose like tears.

Davie walked slowly. The wetness from the ferns was a coolness between his toes, but he did not feel it. The air was fragrant with the scent of meadowsweet and clover. He drew no pleasure from it. At the head of the glen Ben Ulva had doffed its nightcap of sullen clouds and now wore a rose-pink bonnet. Davie didn't even look at it.

Once Joseph sighted a rabbit and went off in instant chase. The rabbit outdistanced him in a matter of seconds. He trotted back to Davie, his long ears swaying gently like the sporran on a Highlander's kilt. To Joseph, though, the whole thing was a mighty triumph. It was his first victory over the enemy. Unless there were rabbits waiting to be chased in heaven, it might well be his last.

As they approached the steep incline, Davie felt his feet suddenly drag in the heather. He knew, with a terrible sureness, what lay beyond it. A frothing, tumbling rush of peat-stained water. The Angus River.

Davie had almost reached the top of the steep hill when he noticed it. The stillness. The queer silence that made the hum of a bee loud in his ear. He stopped, wondering. Something was wrong. Was different. A solitary curlew flew past, trailing its mournful cry behind it. But that was all. Something was missing. Something familiar was gone. Something that belonged here. Then all at once in the sudden silence that closed in after the curlew's cry he knew what it was. He could not hear the Angus!

With a few short bounds he crested the hill. He stopped short. The breath froze in his lungs at the sight that awaited him.

As far as his eyes could see the river was gone!

He stood for almost ten seconds where he was, his mind refusing to accept what his eyes beheld. It was

impossible! The Angus had always been there. Had been there since time began. It was a part of the world itself. Like the sun and the moon and the stars. Its cheery gossip greeted every dawn. Its soft lullaby put every day to bed.

Slowly, as the shock grew less, Davie noticed other things. Although the river was gone, a deep brown channel remained, a channel of still pools and smooth flat rocks. Of long green reeds bending in chocolate-colored mud. Of hundreds of round, white pebbles that gleamed in the sun.

"It's not to be believed at all," he whispered in awe. As if in a trance, he walked across the bed of the river.

The soft mud was a gentle coolness against his bare feet. It must have been like this, he thought, when Moses walked across the Red Sea with the Children of Israel. Only then the waters had been rolled back. Here they had dried up.

Yet of one thing he was certain. God had heard his prayer after all. And He had answered it. True, it *was* a little strange that He had gone to so much trouble to save one little dog's life. But who can tell about prayers anyway?

He watched as Joseph dashed at full speed through the small puddles in the river bed. His skinny little legs seemed to falter as the water broke against him. The next second he would burst through and strut proudly back to Davie, his tail high like a battle standard, his small whiskers coated with glistening drops of moisture.

Davie's heart was light. He had put Joseph into the river just as he had been ordered. He had not disobeyed his father. And Joseph was alive—alive—alive!

He sang as he went home, and he noticed how the world had changed. How dreary it had seemed as he had made his way to the Angus. It couldn't just be the sun, for the sun had been shining before. Only now, somehow, it shone *differently*. With a new warmth and friendliness.

It couldn't be the soft wind that smelled so sweet in his lungs. The wind had been there before. Only like the sun it was different now. The whole world was different now, full of rich gay colors and happy, happy tunes. And as Joseph sported gaily at his heels the song that he had sung that first day came to his lips.

> Will ye no come back again,
> Will ye no, Prince Charlie?
> Better loved ye canna be,
> Will ye no come back again?

And if Bonnie Prince Charlie had "no come back again," at least Joseph had. Back to the world of warm sun and soft hill winds. Back to the world of rabbits to be chased and bones to be buried and ears to be scratched.

Suddenly Davie stopped his whistling. There was something else Joseph was coming back to. Something dark and chilling and fearful.

The world of Ian Campbell.

Ian Campbell stopped when he saw Davie and Joseph. With a big hand he swung the gate closed. With the other he set the wooden milk bucket down hard on the cobbled walk. His brow was black with anger as the boy and dog slowly approached.

"You have disobeyed me, Davie Campbell," he said between tight lips. "Aye, but what is worse, you have broken the word you gave me."

Nell Campbell, alerted by the savage clatter of the milk bucket and the harsh voice of her husband, ran swiftly from the house. She bent down and threw her arms protectively around her son.

"You will not strike the lad, Ian," she said quietly. "I'll take care of this."

The big farmer's eyes flashed. "You will take care of a son who defies his father? A son who breaks his word?" His heavy breathing made his big chest rise and fall, rise and fall. "I am a patient man, Nell Campbell. But I will not be mocked by my own son."

"I did what you said," Davie answered. "Did I not give you my word?"

"Then what brings the dog back?"

Davie looked at his father, then hesitated. All of a sudden he realized something. How strange his story would sound to the ears of another. It takes faith to pray. It takes a stronger faith to believe that a prayer has been answered. His eyes wavered, then fell. He wet his dry lips with his tongue. He stared fixedly at the smooth cobbles. He did not speak.

"Answer me, boy!" thundered Ian Campbell.

Davie gulped and lifted his head. "The Angus was not there at all," he said in a small voice.

"What?"

Even his mother was looking at him queerly. He took a deep breath and went on. "It's all dried up. There's no more Angus. Joseph—he ran all over where it had been."

The tight, white lips separated just wide enough to let the words squeeze through. "And on top of everything else, a liar besides!" His hand shot out and seized Davie roughly by the arm. "How dare you come to me with such lies! How dare you!"

A stab of pain shot up Davie's arm where the fingers bit cruelly into his flesh.

"It's no lie I tell!" he cried. "It's the truth! The truth. The Angus is dried up. Would I tell you if it was not so?"

"Aye, it's the truth Davie speaks. I just heard it now. The workmen on the Government project dammed it up. There's a new lake over by Ben Ulva."

Ian Campbell wheeled around to face the speaker. Murdock stood quietly and looked at his father. No one spoke for fully a minute.

"A new lake?" Ian Campbell finally said. He looked dazed. Slowly the pain slid from his eyes and down his face. Slowly his fingers gave up their fierce grip on Davie's arm. "Then the lad did not lie at all?" he asked in a low voice.

"Is he not your son?" Nell Campbell said quietly.

"Aye," he said slowly, "he is that." He seemed lost in thought. "It will be strange with the Angus gone," he mused after a pause. He spoke as though to himself. "Many a grand day's fishing I had there when I was a lad."

A quick dread chilled Davie's heart. "I hope you're not minding that the Angus is gone!" he cried anxiously. "I only asked for a wee miracle. Honest."

His father was looking at him oddly. So was his mother. So was Murdock.

"Miracle?" Ian Campbell said. "You asked for a miracle?"

"Aye. I did. Last night." He hastened on lest his father would misunderstand. "But only a wee one. I never dreamed that God would be going to all this bother of drying up rivers."

"But why, Davie?" It was almost a cry of anguish. "Why did you want a miracle?"

"It was not for me," Davie answered hurriedly. "It was for Joseph."

"Joseph?" Ian Campbell's face was gray.

Davie nodded. "Aye, it seemed the only way to save

Joseph." Again he looked quickly at his father. "But honest, I asked only for a wee miracle."

For the longest moment Ian Campbell said nothing. And as he stood as though graven in stone, Davie noticed for the first time the depths of the lines around the mouth, the long streaks of silver in the dark hair. His father's voice when he spoke was soft with a softness Davie had never known.

He smiled a little sadly. "Aye, Davie. God answers prayers in many ways. After all, does it not say in the Good Book itself that the Lord moves in a mysterious way His wonders to perform?"

Murdock, who had stood watching the little drama, let a smile flit across his dark face. He ruffled his young brother's red hair. "Now, Davie," he said lightly. "I can understand you having the river dried up and all, but why did you have to start moving mountains around? They must have blasted away half of Ben Ulva when they made that new lake up there."

Davie started. Wasn't that the very thing old Tam Menzies said you could do when you had faith? Davie's mind reeled. How was he to have known what mighty forces he would set free last night when he had prayed for Joseph?

Murdock laughed, then turned to his father.

"They say that the new Government power will be a fine thing for everybody. The electricity will help dry the hay and there will be more fodder for the cattle." He turned and smiled with his eyes at his young brother. "And maybe with better times and all we'll be needing some kind of dog around the place." He scratched his head and looked wryly at Joseph. "*Any* kind of dog."

Davie's heart skipped a beat. Anxiously he looked at his father. There was no expression on the gaunt face. The dark eyes were fixed on where Joseph lay on the cobbled walk, his chin resting trustingly on the farmer's rough boot.

Slowly Ian Campbell's body relaxed. Slowly he bent down. Slowly he drew a big clumsy finger down Joseph's back. "Aye," he said with a soft sigh of resignation, "maybe it's right you are, Murdock. Maybe it's right you are."

The joy in Davie's heart was a winged, soaring thing. Joseph was his! His to keep and to love forever and ever and ever.

He threw himself beside his father and never felt the stones that bruised his bare knees. He watched his father. His own wonderful, kind, understanding father. Somehow the sight of him patting the little dog filled him with a strange and marvelous warmth. And to think that it had been only a few days ago that he had thought he hated this man! Hadn't he been a foolish one! But it was different today. It would *always* be different. Perhaps that was part of the miracle, too.

"And it's a great help he'll be to us," he exulted. "Just wait and see. For it's a grand dog he is with the grand blood in him." He looked at his father. "Am I not right?"

Ian Campbell did not smile often. But he smiled now. A smile at once proud and humble. He put out his arm and pulled his son close to him.

"Aye, the grand blood indeed," he said.

The 7th Pup

by Doris Gates

IN SOME WAYS Billy Bent was a very lucky boy, and he knew it. But in other ways he wasn't so lucky. That's the way it is with nearly everybody, only it was more so with Billy.

First of all Billy loved dogs. What boy doesn't? But Billy loved dogs in a special way. All he really cared about was dogs. He had already decided that when he grew up, he was going to earn his living training them. That wouldn't happen for quite a while, though, because Billy was only nine years old.

But already he had a way with dogs, and an eye for them, too. At least that's what Mr. Riggs said, and he should have known. For Mr. Riggs raised fox terriers and sold them to people who came from miles around to buy them. And Billy lived next door to Mr. Riggs.

The people he lived with were paid by the county to take care of Billy because he was an orphan. That was not lucky. But living next door to Mr. Riggs was. Billy spent most of his time there.

Now one day, Queenie, the best dog at the Riggs' kennel, presented her owner with a litter of puppies. Billy happened to be right at Mr. Riggs' side when he discovered Queenie's new family.

"Well, old lady," Mr. Riggs said kindly, and Queenie wagged her stump of a tail and looked at him with adoring eyes. "How many babies have you this time?"

He moved Queenie out of her box and there, in a black and white heap, were seven puppies cuddled closely together. They were beautiful puppies, with strong, healthy bodies and perfect markings. All but one. He was little and all his markings were in the wrong places. The black spot that should have fitted neatly over his back had slid down on one side. One half of his face was black and the other white. And on the white side he had a black ear, and on the black side a white ear. In short, he couldn't have been more sadly mixed up.

"Well," said Mr. Riggs again, "it won't be hard to decide what to do with that seventh pup." He had put the six good puppies in the box and the seventh was sitting all by himself on the floor of Queenie's pen.

"What do you mean?" asked Billy, but in his heart he knew exactly what Mr. Riggs was going to say.

"Queenie won't have milk for more than six puppies, and that seventh one isn't any good anyway. I'll just have to kill him."

Billy looked at the seventh pup, and all at once he knew that he loved him better than all the rest of Queenie's litter put together. Perhaps it was because the puppy wasn't wanted that made Billy love him so. He could understand how the pup might feel about that, because nobody cared much about him, either.

There is a great difference between having a home of your own and being cared for by people who are paid to do so. Billy always had enough to eat and a good bed to sleep in. Just the same, he knew what it was not to be wanted. So now he wanted the seventh pup. He wanted him more than anything in all the world.

"Yep, I'll have to kill him," Mr. Riggs repeated. "But he's so homely, it won't be much of a loss."

Then Billy spoke. "Don't kill him," he begged. "Give him to me."

Mr. Riggs looked at Billy in surprise. "He's too little to take away from his mother," he said. "You couldn't feed him, son."

"Yes, I could," Billy insisted. "I'll feed him with a baby's bottle. And if he doesn't keep well and strong, then— then, why then I guess you'll have to kill him."

Mr. Riggs could think of nothing to say against Billy's plan, so he gave him the pup. Billy lifted it from the floor while Mr. Riggs held on to Queenie. She didn't care if the puppy was homely, either. Then Mr. Riggs gave Billy one of the nursing bottles which he kept at the kennel for emergencies, and Billy went proudly home, the seventh pup cuddled close in his arms. This was his first dog, and it was the dog among all dogs which he had most wanted for his very own.

The man the county paid for keeping Billy was sitting on the front porch when Billy reached the house. He lowered the paper he was reading to glance at Billy as he

came into sight. He started to raise the paper again when his eyes fell upon the seventh pup.

"Where on earth did you find that?" he demanded, in a voice which said as plain as day that he didn't think much of it.

This was the moment Billy had been waiting for. "How do you like my dog?" he asked.

"What do you mean, *your* dog?" The man's voice had a sharp edge to it now.

"Mr. Riggs just gave him to me for keeps," explained Billy.

"Well, you can just take him right back," said the man. "What made you think you could have a dog?" He gave the paper an angry shake. "Besides, he's about the homeliest mutt I ever had to look at."

"I'll keep him out of sight," begged Billy. "I'll feed him and take care of him and he won't be a bother to anybody."

"Yeah?" said the man. "And who'll pay for his grub? You eat more than your keep right now. There isn't any extra for a dog."

Billy swallowed hard. "He's not a very big dog," he insisted. "He wouldn't eat much and I'll share what's coming to me with him."

"Talk's cheap," said the man, going back to his paper. "You do as I say and take him back to Mr. Riggs."

So Billy turned right around and walked sadly back to the Riggs' place with the pup. But Mr. Riggs wouldn't take him back.

"He's your dog," he told Billy, who was trying to wipe

the tear stains off his cheeks. "When I give a dog, I give him for good."

"But he," Billy nodded toward the house next door, "he won't let me keep him. He won't let me have the food for him and I couldn't let the puppy starve." Billy spoke the words in a shaky voice.

"I haven't said he would starve," said Mr. Riggs. "I only said he was still your dog. How would you like to have him board and room over here?"

"I haven't any money to pay for his keep," explained Billy hopelessly.

"I haven't asked for money," said Mr. Riggs, and smiled. "How would you like to earn the pup's keep?"

Billy looked with surprised eyes at Mr. Riggs. "How?" he asked.

"I've noticed for some time now that you have a way with dogs," Mr. Riggs explained. "I need a little extra help now and then, especially since this new litter arrived. Suppose you come over whenever you get the chance and mix feed and clean the kennels, and I'll board the pup for your pay."

Billy's face broke into a smile so bright that Mr. Riggs couldn't face it and had to look down at the ground for a minute. Would he work for the pup's board! Would he! Why, he'd rather be fussing around dogs than doing anything else in the world, anyway. And just by fussing around dogs, he could keep the pup.

"Gee, Mr. Riggs," he said with a long, happy sigh. "Gee, thanks."

In a couple of days, Mr. Riggs cut off the puppies' tails

because people expected fox terriers to have short tails. But Billy wouldn't let him touch the seventh pup.

"He's so homely, anyway, it won't matter a bit if his tail is too long," he explained. "I don't want him hurt."

"He'll be a funny-looking fox terrier with a too-long tail, all right," said Mr. Riggs. Then he added with a chuckle, "But then, he's funny-looking, anyway."

Billy hadn't listened to a word since Mr. Riggs had said "too-long tail." For the past two days, ever since he had had him, in fact, Billy had been trying to think of a name for his pup. Nothing seemed good enough. Spot, Trixy, Pal. They were all ordinary and none of them seemed to fit. But now, suddenly, Mr. Riggs had given him a name.

"That's it," Billy shouted. "That's his name."

"What's his name?" demanded Mr. Riggs.

"Why, Too-long. It's perfect. He's a dog with a too-long tail, and so Too-long is his own special name."

Mr. Riggs grinned and walked away. And from that day, the seventh pup was known as Too-long.

The weeks passed and then the months. Too-long grew, and his tail grew with him. From the first he thrived on Billy's care. And it seemed as if his too-long tail had been one reason for his good start in life. For while the other puppies were licking their sore stumps and waiting for their shortened tails to heal, Too-long frisked gaily at his master's heels as Billy went faithfully about his kennel chores.

It turned out to be lucky, after all, that the people he lived with didn't care much about Billy. If they had, they might not have wanted him to spend so much time away from home.

As it was, Billy spent more time at the Riggs' place than he did at his own. As soon as school was over, he dashed next door, where Too-long fell upon him with sharp barks of welcome. And whenever Billy had a chance he worked with the pup, teaching him the things a well-trained dog should know. By the time Too-long was six months old, he had learned to follow at Billy's heels, to lie down when told to do so, and to bring a ball right to his master's feet. Even Mr. Riggs had to admit that Too-long, for all his bad looks, was as sharp as a needle.

By the time he was a year old and Billy ten, Too-long stayed wherever you told him to, jumped over a broomstick to bring the ball, spoke, shook hands, and rolled over. Billy thought he was the most wonderful dog in the world.

"You've done a good job with him," Mr. Riggs told Billy. "It's too bad you've taken all that trouble with a dog that can't ever go into the show ring. He could be a champion with what he knows if he just had the looks."

Then, one day just a week before the dog show, bad luck decided to pay a visit to Mr. Riggs. The only dog that he had planned to enter in the show that year took a bad cold. How it happened nobody knew. Mr. Riggs' face looked as long as Too-long's tail.

That's the way it is with the people who own kennels. If they don't have a dog to put in the show, they feel as if the whole year had been lived in vain. Never before, since he had been raising fox terriers, had Mr. Riggs failed to bring home a blue ribbon, which means first prize. And this year, he would have no ribbon at all. Not even a second or a third, which, though they are only yellow and white, are better than no ribbon at all.

Billy, noticing how sad Mr. Riggs looked, began to put his brain to work. He knew a thing or two about dog shows. That very day, with Too-long at his heels, he went downtown to the dog-show office. He didn't say a word about it to Mr. Riggs. But the evening before the show day, he bathed and brushed Too-long within an inch of his life. Then he went over with him again all the things he had taught him. Then he went home, still without saying a word of his plan to anyone.

The next morning, Billy borrowed a collar and rope from the kennel office, and he and Too-long started for the dog show.

Two hours later, Mr. Riggs, wandering about among the barking dogs and crowding people, came at last to the ring where the Obedience Trials were being held. A large crowd was gathered there, for this event was for boys and girls who handled their own dogs, and he had a little trouble at first in seeing what was going on. When at last he could get a view of things, his jaw dropped in astonishment. For there, going through his trials as easily and perfectly as he did in his own back yard, was Too-long. And with him was Billy.

In the ring were other dogs, held a little to one side by their masters while Too-long was having his turn. All kinds of dogs, big and little, fine and homely. But the homeliest of them all was Too-long. Mr. Riggs remembered then that there was one part of every dog show where looks didn't count. That was the Obedience Trials. Just so a dog carried out his master's orders perfectly, nobody cared what he looked like. And if he were perfect enough, he could even win the blue.

Mr. Riggs felt his eyes grow misty as he watched the little dog, his spots all wrong and his tail held out straight and long behind him. There was such an eagerness in the way he tried to do just what Billy wanted that it seemed as if he knew he had a chance of bringing home a prize ribbon today.

Billy was as eager as the dog. He never once looked at the crowd. He never even heard the applause when Too-long jumped the hurdle and brought Billy the make-believe bone. He was too busy trying to send a thought message to Too-long that the hurdle was only a broomstick.

Too-long obeyed every command. Each time this happened, his too-long tail beat his sides in joyful thanks for the attention. The homely little dog had captured the hearts of the audience, as had the boy with the patched jeans.

At last it was over and, after a check-up, a man approached Billy and handed him a blue ribbon. Too-long had won the blue!

Mr. Riggs caught up with Billy outside. "I saw you in there," he said. "I was proud of you."

Billy held out the blue ribbon. "You can put it in the glass box with the others," he said. "The kennel will have a ribbon to show for this year, too. Too-long's blue," he added.

Mr. Riggs took the ribbon. "Thank you, Billy," he said.

"I appreciate what you've just done. Another thing. Too-long is big enough to earn his own keep. He's worth his weight in rats and is every inch a terrier. How would you like to work for wages instead of his board?"

"For you?" asked Billy, a light coming into his face.

"For me," said Mr. Riggs.

"You bet," said Billy. "I'd like that fine."

"Then you're hired as my right-hand man," said Mr. Riggs, and laid his hand on Billy's shoulder. Under it, he could feel Billy pull his shoulders up very straight.

Ahead of them, Too-long frisked and galloped, his too-long tail wagging happily. It is doubtful if he knew any more than did Billy that seven is really a very, very lucky number!

The Christmas Hunt

by Borden Deal

IT SHOULD HAVE BEEN the best Christmas of them all, that year at Dog Run. It started out to be, anyway. I was so excited, watching my father talking on the telephone, that I couldn't stand still. For I was ten years old and I had never been on a quail shoot in my whole life. I wanted to go on the big Christmas Day hunt even more than I wanted that bicycle I was supposed to get. And I really needed the bicycle to cover with speed and ease the two miles I had to walk to school.

The Christmas Day hunt was always the biggest and best of the season. It was almost like a field trial; only the best hunters and the finest dogs were invited by my father. All my life I had been hearing great tales of past Christmas Day hunts. And now I knew with a great ten-year-old certainty that I was old enough to go.

My father hung up the phone and turned around, grinning. "That was Walter," he said. "There'll be ten of them this year. And Walter is bringing his new dog. If all he claims for that dog is true—"

"Papa," I said.

"Lord," my mother said. "That'll be a houseful to feed."

My father put his arm around her shoulders, hugging her. "Oh, you know you like it," he said. "They come as much for your cooking as they do for the hunting, I think."

My mother pursed her lips in the way she had, and then smiled. "Wild turkey," she said. "You think you could shoot me four or five nice fat wild turkeys?"

I wanted to jump up and down to attract attention. But that was kid stuff, a tactic for the five-year-olds, though I had to admit it was effective. But I was ten. So I said, "Papa."

My father laughed. "I think I can," he said. "I'll put in a couple of mornings trying."

"Papa," I said desperately.

"Wild turkey stuffed with wild rice," my mother said quickly, thoughtfully, in her planning voice. "Giblet gravy, mashed potatoes, maybe a nice potato salad—"

"If I don't fail on the turkeys," my father said.

"Papa!" I said.

My father turned to me. "Come on, Tom," he said. "We've got to feed those dogs."

That's the way parents are, even when you're ten years old. They can talk right on and never hear a word you say. I ran after my father as he left the kitchen, hoping for a chance to get my words in edgewise. But my father was walking fast and already the clamor of the bird dogs was rising up to cover any speech I might want to make.

The dogs were standing on the wire fence in long dappled rows, their voices lifted in greeting. Even in my urgent need I had to stop and admire them. There's nothing prettier in the whole world than a good bird dog. There's a nobleness to its head, an intelligence in its eyes, that no other animal has. Just looking at them sent a shiver down my backbone; and the thought of shooting birds over them—well, the shiver just wasn't in my backbone now, I was shaking all over.

All of the dogs except one were in the same big run. But my father kept Calypso Baby in her own regal pen. I went to her and looked into her soft brown eyes. She stood up tall on the fence, her strong, lithe body stretched to its full height, as tall as I was.

"Hello, Baby," I whispered, and she wagged her tail. "You gonna find me some birds this Christmas, Baby? You gonna hunt for me like you do for Papa?"

She lolled her tongue, laughing at me. We were old friends. Calypso Baby was the finest bird dog in that part of the country. My father owned a number of dogs and kept and trained others for his town friends. But Calypso Baby was his personal dog, the one that he took to the field trials, the one he shot over in the big Christmas Day hunt held at Dog Run.

My father was bringing the sack of feed from the shed. I put out my hand, holding it against the wire so Calypso Baby could lick my fingers.

"This year," I whispered to her. "This year I'm going." I left Calypso Baby, went with determination toward my father. "Papa," I said, in a voice not to be denied this time.

My father was busy opening the sack of dog food.

"Papa," I said firmly, "I want to talk to you." It was the tone and the words my father used often toward me, so much of mimicry that my father looked down at me in surprise, at last giving me his attention.

"What is it?" he said. "What do you want?"

"Papa, I'm ten years old," I said.

My father laughed. "Well, what of it?" he said. "Next year you'll be eleven. And the next year twelve."

"I'm old enough to go on the Christmas hunt," I said.

Incredibly, my father laughed. "At ten?" he said. "I'm afraid not."

I stood, stricken. "But—" I said.

"No," my father said, in the voice that meant No, and no more talking about it. He hoisted the sack of feed and took it into the wire dog pen, the bird dogs crowding around him, rearing up on him in their eagerness.

"Well, come on and help me," my father said impatiently. "I've got a lot of things to do."

Usually I enjoyed the daily feeding of the dogs. But not today; I went through the motions dumbly, silently, not paying any attention to the fine bird dogs crowding around me. I cleaned the watering troughs with my usual care, but my heart was not in it.

After the feeding was over, I scuffed stubbornly about my other tasks and then went up to my room, not even coming down when my father came home at dusk excited with the two wild turkeys he had shot. I could hear him talking to my mother in the kitchen, and the ring of their voices had already the feel of Christmas, a hunting cheer that made them brighter, livelier, than usual. But none of the cheer and the pleasure came into me, even though Christmas was almost upon us and yesterday had been the last day of school.

That night I hunted. In my dreams I was out ahead of all the other men and dogs, Calypso Baby quartering the field in her busy way, doing it so beautifully I ached inside to watch her. All the men and dogs stopped their own hunting to watch us, as though it were a field trial. When Calypso Baby pointed, I raised the twelve-gauge shotgun, moved in on her on the ready, and Calypso Baby flushed the birds in her fine, steady way. They came up in an explosive whir, and I had the gun to my shoulder, squeezing off the shot just the way I'd been told to do. Three quail dropped like stones out of the covey and I swung the gun, following a single. I brought down the single with the second barrel, and Calypso Baby was already bringing the first bird to me in her soft, unbruising mouth. I knelt to pat her for a moment, and Baby whipped her tail to tell me how fine a shot I was, how much she liked for me to be the one shooting over her today.

Soon there was another covey, and I did even better on this one, and then another and another, and nobody was hunting at all, not even my father, who was laughing and grinning at the other men, knowing this was his boy, Tom, and his dog, Calypso Baby, and just full of pride with it all. When it was over, the men crowded around and patted me on the shoulder, hefting the full game bag in admiration, and then there was my father's face close before me, saying, "I was wrong, son, when I said a ten-year-old boy isn't old enough to go bird hunting with the best of us."

Then I was awake and my father, dressed in his hunting clothes, was shaking me, and it was morning. I looked up dazedly into his face, unable to shake off the dream, and I knew what it was I had to do. I had to show my father. Only then would he believe.

"Are you awake?" my father said. "You'll have to change the water for the dogs. I'm going to see if I can get some more turkeys this morning."

"All right," I said. "I'm awake now."

My father left. I got up and ate breakfast in the kitchen, close to the warm stove. I didn't say anything to my mother about my plans. I went out and watered the dogs as soon as the sun was up, but I didn't take the time, as I usually did, to play with them.

"Me and you are going hunting," I told Calypso Baby as I changed her water. She jumped and quivered all over, knowing the word as well as I did.

I went back into the house, listening for my mother. She was upstairs, making the beds. I went into the spare room where my father kept all the hunting gear. I was trembling, remembering the dream, as I went to the gun rack and touched the cold steel of the double-barreled twelve-gauge. But I knew it would be very heavy for me. I took the single-barrel instead, though I knew that pretty near ruined my chances for a second shot unless I could reload very quickly.

I picked up a full shell bag and hung it under my left arm. I found a game bag and hung it under my right arm. The strap was too long and the bag dangled emptily to my knees, banging against me as I walked. I tied a knot in the strap so the bag would rest comfortably on my right hip. The gun was heavy in my hands as I walked into the hallway, listening for my mother. She was still upstairs.

"Mamma, I'm gone," I shouted up to her. "I'll be back in a little while." That was so she wouldn't be looking for me.

"All right," she called. "Don't wander far off. Your father will be back in an hour or two and might have something for you to do."

I hurried out of the house, straight to Calypso Baby's den. I did not look up, afraid that my mother might be watching out of the window. That was a danger I could do nothing about, so I just ignored it. I opened the gate to Baby's pen and she came out, circling and cavorting.

"Come on, Baby," I whispered. "Find me some birds now. Find me a whole lot of birds."

We started off, circling the barn so we would not be seen from the house and going straight away in its shadow as far as we could. Beyond the pasture we crossed a cornfield, Calypso Baby arrowing straight for the patch of sedgegrass beyond. Her tail was whiplike in its thrash, her head high as she plunged toward her work, and I had to hurry to keep up. The gun was clumsy in my hands and the two bags banged against my hips. But I remembered not to run with the gun, remembered to keep the breech open until I was ready to shoot. I knew all about hunting; I just hadn't had a chance to practice what I knew. When I came home with a bag full of fine birds my father would have to admit that I knew how to hunt, that I was old enough for the big

Christmas Day hunt when all the great hunters came out from town for the biggest day of the season.

When I ducked through the barbed-wire fence Calypso Baby was waiting for me, standing a few steps into the sedgegrass, her head up watching me alertly. Her whole body quivered with her eagerness to be off. I swept my arm in the gesture I had seen my father use so many times and Calypso Baby plunged instantly into the grass. She was a fast worker, quartering back and forth with an economical use of her energy. She could cover a field in half the time it took any other dog. The first field was empty, and we passed on to the second one. Somehow Calypso Baby knew that birds were here. She steadied down, hunting slowly, more thoroughly.

Then, startling me though I had been expecting it, she froze into a point, one foot up, her tail straight back, her head flat with the line of her backbone. I froze too. I couldn't move, I couldn't even remember to breech the gun and raise it to my shoulder. I stood as still as the dog, all of my knowledge flown out of my head, and yet far back under the panic I knew that the birds weren't going to hold, they were going to rise in just a moment. Calypso Baby, surprised at my inaction, broke her point to look at me in inquiry. Her head turned toward me and she asked the question as plain as my father's voice: *Well, what are you going to do about these fine birds I found for you?*

I could move then. I took a step or two, fumblingly breeched the gun, raised it to my shoulder. The birds rose of their own accord in a sudden wild drum of sound. I yanked at the trigger, unconsciously bracing myself against the blast and the recoil. Nothing happened. Nothing at all happened. I tugged at the trigger wildly, furiously, but it was too late and the birds were gone.

I lowered the gun, looking down at it in bewilderment. I had forgotten to release the safety. I wanted to cry at my own stupidity, I could feel the tears standing in my eyes. This was not at all like my dream of last night, when I and the dog and the birds had all been so perfect.

Calypso Baby walked back to me and looked up into my face. I could read the puzzled contempt in her eyes. She lay down at my feet, putting her muzzle on her paws. I looked down at her, ashamed of myself and knowing that she was ashamed. She demanded perfection, just as my father did.

"It was my fault, Baby," I told her. I leaned over and patted her on the head. "You didn't do anything wrong. It was me."

I started off then, looking back at the bird dog. She did not follow me. "Come on," I told her. "Hunt."

She got up slowly and went out ahead of me again. But she worked in a puzzled manner, checking back to me frequently. She no longer had the joy, the confidence, with which she had started out.

"Come on, Baby," I coaxed her. "Hunt, Baby. Hunt."

We crossed into another field, low grass this time, and when we found the covey there was very little time for setting myself. Calypso Baby pointed suddenly; I jerked the gun to my shoulder, remembering the safety this time, and then Calypso Baby flushed the birds. They rose up before me and I pulled the trigger, hearing the blast of the gun, feeling the shock of it into my shoulder knocking me back a step.

But not even one bird dropped like a fateful stone out of the covey. The covey had gone off low and hard on an angle to the left, and I had completely missed the shot, aiming straight ahead instead of swinging with the birds. Calypso Baby did not even attempt to point singles. She dropped her head and her tail and started away from me, going back toward the house.

I ran after her, calling her, crying now but with anger rather than hurt. Baby would never like me again, she would hold me in the indifference she felt toward any person who was not a bird hunter. She would tolerate me as she tolerated my mother, and the men who came out with shiny new hunting clothes and walked all over the land talking about how the dogs didn't hold the birds properly so you could get a decent shot.

I couldn't be one of those. I ran after the dog, calling her, until at last she suffered me to come near. I knelt, fondling her head, talking to her, begging her for another chance.

"I'll get some birds next time," I told her. "You just watch. You hear?"

At last, reluctantly, she consented to hunt again. I followed her, my hands gripping the heavy gun, determined this time. I knew it was my last chance; she would not give me another. I could not miss this time.

We hunted for an hour before we found another covey of birds. I was tired, the gun and the frustration heavier with every step. But, holding only last night's dream in my mind, I refused to quit. At last Calypso Baby froze into a beautiful point. I could feel myself sweating, my teeth gritted hard. I had to bring down a bird this time.

It seemed to be perfect. I had plenty of time but I hurried anyway, just to be sure. Then the birds were rising in a tight cluster and I was pulling the trigger before I had the heavy gun lined up—and in the midst of the thundering blast I heard Calypso Baby yell with pain as the random shot tore into her hip.

I threw down the gun and ran toward her, seeing the blood streaking down her leg as she staggered away from me, whimpering. I knelt, trying to coax her to me, but she was afraid. I was crying, feeling the full weight of the disaster. I had committed the worst crime of any bird hunter; I had shot my own dog.

Calypso Baby was trying to hide in a clump of bushes. She snapped at me in her fear when I reached in after her, but I did not feel the pain in my hand. I knelt over her, looking at the shredded hip. It was a terrible wound, I could see only blood and raw flesh. I snatched off the empty hunting bag I had donned so optimistically, the shell bag, and took off my coat. I wrapped her in the coat and picked her up in my arms. She was very heavy, hurting, whining with each jolting step as I ran toward the house.

I came into the yard doubled over with the catch in my side from the running, and my legs were trembling. My father was sitting on the back porch with three wild turkeys beside him, cleaning his gun. He jumped to his feet when he saw the wounded dog.

"What happened?" he said. "Did some fool hunter shoot her?"

I stopped, standing before my father and holding the wounded dog; I looked into his angry face. They were the most terrible words I had ever had to say. "I shot her, Papa," I said.

My father stood very still. I did not know what would happen. I had never done anything so bad in my whole life and I could not even guess how my father would react. The only thing justified would be to wipe me off the face of the earth with one irate gesture of his hand.

I gulped, trying to move the pain in my throat out of the way of the words. "I took her out bird hunting," I said. "I wanted to show you—if I got a full bag of birds, I thought you'd let me go on the Christmas Day hunt—"

"I'll talk to you later," my father said grimly, taking the dog from me and starting into the kitchen. "I've got to try to save this dog's life now."

I started into the kitchen behind my father. He turned. "Where's the gun you shot her with?" he said.

"I—left it."

"Don't leave it lying out there in the field," my father said in a stern voice.

I wanted very badly to go into the kitchen, find out that the dog would live. But I turned, instead, and went back the way I had come, walking with my head down, feeling shrunken inside myself. I had overreached; I had risen up today full of pride beyond my ability, and in the stubbornness of the pride I had been blind until the terrible accident had opened my eyes so that I could see myself clearly—too clearly. I found the gun, the two bags, where I had dropped them. I picked them up without looking at the smear of blood where Calypso had lain. I went back to the house slowly, not wanting to face it, reluctant to see the damage I had wrought.

When I came into the kitchen, my father had the dog stretched out on the kitchen table. My mother stood by his side with bandages and ointment in her hands. The wound was cleaned of the bird shot and dirt and blood. Calypso Baby whined when she saw me and I felt my heart cringe with the rejection.

My father looked at me across the dog. The anger was gone out of him, his voice was slow and searching and not to be denied. "Now I want to know why you took my gun and my dog without permission," he said.

"David," my mother said to him.

My father ignored her, kept his eyes hard on my face. I knew it wouldn't do any good to look toward my mother. This was between me and my father, and there was no refuge for me anywhere in the world. I didn't want a refuge; I knew I had to face not only my father, but myself.

"I—I wanted to go on the Christmas Day hunt," I said again. "I thought if I—" I stopped. It was all that I had to say; it seemed pretty flimsy to me now.

My father looked down at the dog. I was surprised at the lack of anger in him. I could read only sadness in his voice. "She may be ruined for hunting," he said. "Even if the wound heals good, if she doesn't lose the use of her leg, she may be gun-shy for the rest of her life. At best, I'll never be able to show her in field trials again. You understand what you've done?"

"Yes, sir," I said. I wanted to cry. But that would not help, any more than anger from my father would help.

"You see now why I said you weren't old enough?" my father said. "You've got to be trained for hunting, just like a dog is trained. Suppose other men had been out there, suppose you had shot a human being?"

"David!" my mother said.

My father turned angrily toward her. "He's got to learn!" he said. "There's too many people in this world trying to do things without learning how to do them first. I don't want my boy to be one of them."

"Papa," I said. "I'm—I'm sorry. I wouldn't have hurt Calypso Baby for anything in the world."

"I'm not going to punish you," my father said. He looked down at the dog. "This is too bad for a whipping to settle. But I want you to think about today. I don't want you to put it out of your mind. You knew that when the time came ripe for it, I intended to teach you, take you out like I'd take a puppy, and hunt with you. After a while, you could hunt by yourself. Then if you were good enough—and only if you were good enough—you could go on the Christmas Day hunt. The Christmas Day hunt is the place you come to, not the place you start out from. Do you understand?"

"Yes, sir," I said. I would have been glad to settle for a whipping. But I knew that a mere dusting of the breeches would be inadequate for my brashness, my overconfidence, for the hurt I had given not only to the fine bird dog but also to my father—and to myself.

"You've got to take special care of Calypso Baby," my father said. "Maybe if you take care of her yourself while she's hurt, she'll decide to be your friend again."

I looked at the dog and I could feel the need of her confidence and trust. "Yes, sir," I said. Then I said humbly, "I hope she will be friends with me again."

I went toward the hall, needing to be alone in my room. I stopped at the kitchen doorway, looked back at my father and mother watching me. I had to say it in a hurry if I was going to say it at all.

"Papa," I said, the words rushing softly in my throat, threatening to gag there before I could get them out. "I—I don't think I deserve that bicycle this Christmas. I don't deserve it at all."

My father nodded his head. "All right, son," he said gravely. "This is your own punishment for yourself."

"Yes," I said, forcing the word, the loss empty inside me and yet feeling better too. I turned and ran out of the room and up the stairs.

Christmas came, but without any help from me at all. I went to bed on Christmas Eve heavy with the knowledge that tomorrow morning there would be no shiny new bicycle under the tree, there would be no Christmas Day hunt for me. I couldn't prevent myself from waking up at the usual excited time, but I made myself turn over and go back to sleep. When I did, reluctantly, go downstairs, the Christmas tree did not excite me, nor the usual gifts I received every year, the heavy sweater, the gloves, the scarf, the two new pairs of blue jeans. I just wouldn't let myself think about the bicycle.

After my father had gone outside, my mother hugged me to her in a sudden rush of affection. "He would have given you the bicycle anyway," she said. "If you hadn't told him you didn't want it."

I looked up at her. "I didn't deserve it," I said. "Maybe next year I will."

She surprised me then by holding me and crying. I

heard the first car arrive outside, the voices of the men excited with the promise of hunting. My mother stood up and said briskly, "Well, this is not getting that big dinner cooked," and went into the kitchen without looking back.

I went out on the front porch. It was perfect quail-hunting weather, cold but not too cold, with a smoky haze lying over the earth. The dogs knew that today was for hunting; I could hear them from around behind the house, standing on the wire fence in broad-shouldered rows, their voices yelping and calling. All except Calypso Baby. All except me.

I stood aside, watching the men arrive in their cars, my father greeting them. Their breaths hung cloudy in the air and they moved with a sharp movement to their bodies. These were the best hunters in the whole country-side, and today would be a great comradeship and competition. Any man invited on this hunt could be proud of the invitation alone.

I felt almost remote as I watched, as I went with them around the side of the house to the dogs. They all went to examine Calypso Baby, and I felt a freezing inside; but my father only said, "She got shot by accident," and did not tell the whole terrible story.

Then my father looked at his watch and said, "Let's wait a few more minutes. Walter ought to be here soon. Hate to start without him."

One of the men called, "Here he comes now," and Walter drove up in his battered car.

"Come here, son," my father said, speaking to me for the first time this morning, and I went reluctantly to his side. I was afraid it was coming now, the whole story, and all the men would look at me in the same way that Calypso Baby had after I had shot her.

My father drew me to the side of Walter's car, reached in, and brought out a basket. "You wanted a bicycle," he said. "Then you decided yourself you should wait. Because you made the decision yourself, I decided you were old enough for this."

I looked at the bird-dog puppy in the basket. All of a sudden Christmas burst inside me like a skyrocket, out of the place where I had kept it suppressed all this time.

"Papa," I said. "Papa—"

"Take him," my father said.

I reached into the basket and took out the puppy. The puppy licked my chin with his harsh warm tongue. He was long, gangly, his feet and head too big for his body —but absolutely beautiful.

My father knelt beside me, one hand on the puppy. "I told Walter to bring me the finest bird-dog puppy he could find," he said. "He's kin to Calypso Baby; he's got good blood."

"Thank you, Papa," I said in a choking voice. "I—I'd rather have him than the bicycle. I'll name him Calypso Boy, I'll—"

"When this puppy is ready for birds, we'll train him," my father said. "While we train the puppy, we'll train you too. When the time comes, you can both go on the Christmas Day hunt—if you're good enough."

"We'll be good enough," I said. "Both of us will be good enough."

"I hope so," my father said. He stood up and looked at the men standing around us, all of them smiling down at me and Calypso Boy. "Let's go," he said. "Those birds are going to get tired of waiting on us."

They laughed and hollered, and the dogs moiled and sounded in the excitement as they were let out of the pen. They fanned out across the pasture, each man or two men taking a dog. I stood watching, holding the puppy warm in my arms. I looked at Calypso Baby, standing crippled in her pen looking longingly after the hunters. I went over and spoke to her. She whined; then for the first time since the accident she wagged her tail at me.

I looked down at the puppy in my arms. "We'll be going," I told him, as he licked at my chin. "One of these days, when you're a dog and I'm a man, we'll be right out there with the best of them."

It was three years more before I got to go on my first Christmas hunt. Papa had been right, of course. In the time between I had learned a great deal myself while training Calypso Boy to hunt. With the good blood in him he turned out to be a great bird dog—second only, I guess, to Calypso Baby, who recovered well from her wound and was Papa's dog the day Calypso Boy and I made our first Christmas hunt.

But of all the Christmases, before and since, I guess I remember best the one when Calypso Baby was hurt— and Calypso Boy first came to me.

The Strange Dog

by Russell Gordon Carter

ON THE LONG BARE RIBBON of beach half a mile from his home, Michael Johnson halted abruptly, his blue eyes wide with surprise. In front of him in the moist sand that bordered the great salt marshes stretched a line of fresh footprints so far apart that he wondered what kind of animal could have made them.

As he bent closer he said to himself, "Could it have been a dog?" And then he remembered the book he had been reading just before his mother and father went to the city for the afternoon. It was a book about a boy who owned a big dog, and when he had finished reading it he had exclaimed, "Oh, I wish I owned a dog!" Then his father had said, "Yes, Michael, soon we must get a dog." And his mother had added, "A nice big dog!"

Still wondering about the footprints, Michael followed them up the lonely beach toward the little rotting wharf where he and his father owned a small rowboat. Halfway to the wharf he came to a place where there were a great many of the footprints, and among them he made out the

146

footprints of a man. They were all mixed up and very close together, as if something exciting had happened there. While he was trying to think what it could have been he noticed a short length of chain gleaming in the sand, and as he reached for it he saw it was part of a dog collar.

Suddenly, far up the beach, he spied something coming swiftly toward him. Again he stood with eyes wide, his heart pounding, knowing now for certain what had made the footprints—a dog, the biggest dog he had ever seen! It was like a greyhound but much heavier, and as it came racing toward him, it seemed to be exactly the color of the low smoke-gray autumn sky. Michael stood motionless, his hands clenched in front of him, noting the dog's long narrow head, the small pointed ears and the hard rough hair that covered the young powerful body.

Within a few paces of the boy the dog halted, head lifted, nostrils sniffing. For several seconds the two of them looked at each other. Then Michael put out a hand and said gently, "Come here, boy!"

The dog hesitated, moving his long curved tail from side to side. Then he came slowly forward. When he was within arm's length, his muzzle was on a level with the boy's chin. Michael smiled and stroked the bony head, running his fingers lightly around a recent bruise near one ear. All the while the dog looked at him out of dark friendly eyes. As the boy slipped an arm around the thick arching neck and felt the warm body against him, he knew that never in his life had he wanted anything so much as he wanted this dog!

"You're my dog," he said, and fumbled in his pocket for a cookie. The dog sniffed it, his mouth opened, and the cookie was gone. He wagged his tail and cocked his head hopefully, and again Michael fumbled in his pocket. As the dog swallowed the last of the cookies, Michael said to himself, "Somebody once owned him, but now he belongs to me!" Nevertheless, he knew he was only pretending. . . .

It was a strange kind of day, with ragged clouds scurrying northward and a restless feeling in the air—a day in which it was easy to pretend. Side by side, Michael and the dog followed the curve of the shore to where the sea came in like a great green-and-silver serpent through the marshes. There against a sagging wharf built of whitened driftwood the little rowboat floated motionless among the high grasses. Michael climbed on to the wharf and sat down, and the dog squatted beside him, head raised, watching the gulls screaming above the dark marshland. A green fly alighted on the wharf, and he snapped at it.

"You didn't get it, did you, boy?" Michael said, and laughed. He caught hold of the frayed rope fastened to the boat and drew the craft toward him. He wouldn't go out in it, of course, without his father—and, anyway, the oars were up at the house—but it would be all right to sit in it. When it was against the wharf, he slid his legs downward and then let go. Seated in the stern, he called, "Come, boy, get in with me!"

The dog lowered his head uncertainly, snapped at another green fly, lowered his head again—and then jumped.

"Hey!" Michael cried, clutching the sides while the boat pitched and rocked. "You almost upset us!" He looked at the upper part of the rope hanging limp against the wharf. "See, you broke the rope!"

But it didn't matter. The boat floated motionless again, its bow deep among the grasses. Putting an arm around the dog, Michael closed his eyes. With the water gently lapping, and the smell of the sea in his nostrils, and the wind singing in his ears, he imagined the tall marsh grass slipping swiftly past on either side of him. "You're my dog," he whispered, "and we're going on a long voyage together!"

When he opened his eyes he was startled at sight of the familiar grass tops still hanging over the bow of the motionless boat.

The dog rose and thrust his head over the side, causing the boat to rock. He began to drink, but soon lifted his head and shook the water off. Then he thrust his muzzle into the water on the other side—and again lifted his head and shook the water off.

"You're awfully thirsty, aren't you?" Michael said. "Well, I'm thirsty too!" A battered tin pail lay in the bottom, and picking it up, he said, "You stay here, boy, and I'll get some nice fresh water for you."

He climbed upward onto the wharf and hesitated as the dog prepared to follow him. "I don't want him to come with me," he said to himself and looked at the bruise on the dog's head. "Maybe somebody hit him," he thought, remembering the footprints all mixed up. "If I let him come with me, maybe the man who hit him will see him, and then I'll lose him!" Hauling off his sweater, he tossed it into the boat. "You take care of it, boy," he said. "I'll soon be back."

The dog sniffed the sweater and looked up at him.

"Take care of it," Michael repeated. "That's right!" he added as the dog lay down again with one paw buried in the folds of the sweater. . . .

Swinging the pail, Michael hurried across rolling pasture land toward a low, red-roofed house a long way off. He knew the house. It was a small quick-lunch restaurant, and there was a sign on it that read, "Ed's Place." He also knew Mr. Ed Allen, the owner, a big man with a bald head and a round smiling face. . . .

"Well, how are ye?" Ed exclaimed as the boy entered. He laid aside the newspaper he had been reading. "Haven't seen you in a long time! What can I do for ye?"

"I'd like a drink of water, please," Michael said.

"Is that all!" Ed reached behind the long counter and filled a glass.

When Michael had finished drinking he asked, "Now may I please have some water in this pail?"

Ed lifted his thin eyebrows. "What ye want it for?"

"For a dog," Michael said.

"Your dog? Didn't know ye had one!" Ed looked surprised.

Michael wanted to say, "Yes, he's my dog!" But with Ed looking straight at him, he couldn't pretend. So he set the pail on the counter and was silent.

"Funny thing," Ed said over his shoulder while he was filling the pail, "a man was in here about an hour ago, lookin' for a dog he'd lost—"

Michael felt his breath come quickly.

"A big dog, worth money," Ed went on. "Irish wolf-hound, biggest hunting dog there is. Man had part of a dog collar. Broke it, tryin' to put it on. Dog didn't want to wear a collar an' ran away. So if you own a big dog, my boy, you be careful. Some dogs don't like to wear collars. I wouldn't if I was a dog—"

Michael swallowed hard while his hand reached into his pocket and closed on the piece of chain he had picked up on the beach. . . .

Ed passed the pail of water across the counter and added, "The man said he'd be back later, but as fer me, I don't care whether he finds the dog or not, because he didn't look to me like the kind of man who ought to own a dog. I mean—"

But just then a group of people came in, and Ed had to make up sandwiches for them. . . .

Michael hurried out the door and set off down the road and thence to the beach. The sky had darkened within the past half hour, and the heavy gray clouds looked lower than any clouds he had ever seen. There were no gulls now, and the only sounds were the singing of the wind in his ears and the creaking of the wire handle on the pail.

Within sight of the wharf, he called, "Hi, boy, here I am! Some nice water for you!" He waited for the dog to jerk his head upward from the bottom of the boat, but nothing happened.

Michael ran forward, slopping some of the water onto his legs. "Hi!" he called again. "Water!" Then he stopped short. The boat was empty.

He ran out onto the wharf and turned his head this way

and that, gazing far up and down the beach and across the fields. "Where are you, boy?" he shouted. "You're my dog—yes, you are! Please, come back!" And he clapped his hands above the whistling of the wind . . . but nothing moved either on the beach or in the fields beyond.

In the moist sand in front of the wharf he could see the dog's footprints leading toward the distant pasture land. He followed them until they lost themselves where the sand was dry and soft and deep. Then he returned to the wharf and, lowering himself into the boat, picked up the sweater. As he fastened the arms of it around his neck he said to himself, "He didn't run away from me, he wouldn't! He just went off to look for water."

But his eyes suddenly hurt, and he closed them tight. A strong puff of wind thrust the boat sidewise, and the ripples drummed and sang against the wood. Michael sat motionless, cold hands gripping the seat, thinking of the dog . . . his dog. . . .

As a much stronger puff of wind thrust hard at the boat, the boy opened his eyes. To his surprise, the tall grass on either side of him was slipping swiftly past just as earlier he had imagined it. He twisted about on the seat, and there was the wharf half a dozen yards astern and growing rapidly smaller. Leaning far out, he snatched at the moving grass stems, but they either broke or slid through his fingers, cutting the skin. . . . And then, a moment later, the grass was too far away for him to clutch at it.

Lifting his head, he shouted against the strong south wind. Again and again he shouted while the wharf grew smaller and smaller in the distance. . . . At last he turned and sat with hands clutching the side of the boat. The channel broadened, and here and there he noticed patches of dead grass moving along beside him on the outgoing tide. Part of an old lobster crate came floating along, and he reached for it, thinking he might use it as a paddle, but it was just a few inches farther than the tips of his straining fingers. Presently he saw it drift toward one side of the channel. Then he lost sight of it altogether. . . .

Ahead of him now he glimpsed the open sea, deep purple where it met the pale gray horizon. Looking at it, he felt his eyes begin to hurt again, but this time he didn't close them. Facing toward the land, he began once more to shout. With his hands cupped around his mouth, he shouted until his voice was hoarse and his throat ached. . . . And all the while the boat drifted nearer and nearer the open sea. . . .

The wharf now was so far away it looked no larger than an old broken gray box the tide might have washed up. While Michael stared at it, struggling against the wish to close his eyes and pretend that everything was just a dream, he saw something moving toward him . . . something in the broad channel between himself and the wharf . . . something small and dark and glistening like the head of one of the seals he had sometimes seen on the rocks far to the north where the marshes ended. . . .

At first he thought it really was a seal. Then as he pushed himself as high as possible on the seat he uttered a cry of joy. The dog! "Come on, boy!" he shouted, and clapped his hands encouragingly. "Come on, boy!"

Slowly the dog drew nearer and nearer the drifting boat. Now Michael could see the upthrust nose and the shining ripples that made a widening arrowhead on the gray and silver water. Now he could see the eyes and the flattened glistening ears. "Good old boy!" he shouted.

When the dog was within a few feet of the boat, Michael reached forth a welcoming hand. Then he patted the dark dripping head as it came to rest against the low gunwale. Gazing downward, the boy forgot the open sea and his fear of it. "Here," he said, seizing the broken rope fastened to the bow. "Here, take it!" And he thrust it at the dog. "Catch hold now and swim! Swim back to the wharf!"

The dog's mouth opened and then closed on the rope, but the head remained resting against the gunwale.

"Swim, boy!" Michael repeated, but the dog made no movement.

Michael threw a swift glance over his shoulder, and suddenly his fear returned. Out there beyond the edge of the marshes he could see great waves breaking white against a long black reef. He even imagined he heard the sound of them; an angry, threatening sound.

"Swim, boy, please swim!" he pleaded, but with teeth still clamped on the rope, the dog blinked up at him, bewildered, inquiring. . . .

Once more Michael looked toward the open sea, and now he was sure he could hear the angry crash and hiss of waves against the reef. Even a big ship striking that great mass of black rock would go to pieces, and the small boat seemed to be drifting straight toward it! The wind was growing stronger, blowing cold against his lips and eyelids, fluttering the sweater draped across his shoulders. He clenched his teeth and swallowed hard, once more fighting the desire to close his eyes and pretend that everything was just a dream.

Overhead a solitary gull flashed white against heavy ragged clouds. In the water, with head still against the gunwale, the dog sniffed upward and blinked his eyes. And in the boat, helplessly drifting, Michael sat with lips parted and trembling, staring over his shoulder at the vast open sea and the long, black reef where great waves broke white. . . .

Something had happened to the boat! It was no longer drifting. Michael could hear the sudden music of ripples against the side and then the faint creak of the rope. Jerking his head around, away from the open sea, he uttered a cry of joy. The dog was swimming!

Breathless, Michael watched him. Steadily the dog swam, head a little on one side, jaws fastened upon the rope and steadily, while the ripples beat against the wood, the boat moved slowly toward the little wharf that still looked no larger than an old broken gray box.

Could the dog swim as far as that, towing the boat, Michael asked himself? "He's strong, but the tide is against him, and maybe he can't do it!" he murmured. "Oh, I wish I could help!"

But there seemed nothing to do except sit and watch while the small head nosed its way through the water and the rope tightened and slackened and the wind bent the green grass tops and turned them to silver. As wisps and patches of dead grass skimmed past, the boat seemed

to be moving at great speed . . . but it was a long time before it reached the narrow part of the channel where high walls of waving green rose on either side. . . .

The afternoon light was fading when Michael spied a short flat piece of driftwood floating toward him. Reaching far outward, as he had reached for the piece of lobster crate, he drew it over the gunwale. "Just what I want!" he exclaimed, and began to paddle with it. "See, now I'm helping you, boy!"

Here in the narrow channel the water was smooth and dark. Ahead the wharf no longer looked like an old broken gray box. It was larger, and beyond it Michael could see the gray sand and the rolling purple pasture land. . . .

Twilight was closing in when at last the boat thrust its prow into the grass alongside the wharf. As Michael caught hold of the dangling rope and tied the other length to it, the dog splashed ashore and dropped upon

his side, eyes closed, long legs outstretched, ribs heaving.
"You're tired, aren't you?" Michael murmured. . . . On
the wharf, he picked up the partly filled pail and carried
it ashore. "Here," he said, "here's the fresh water I got
for you!"

The dog rose slowly and drank and drank and drank
until the pail was empty. Then Michael flung his arms
around him. "You're my dog!" he cried. "More than ever
you're my dog! You saved my life, and I'll never, never,
never let you go! Mom and Daddy will love you!" Yet
even as he spoke he remembered what Ed had said: "A
man was in here about an hour ago, lookin' for a dog he'd
lost . . . said he'd be back later. . . .

Once more Michael's eyes suddenly began to hurt, and
the hurt increased and became almost unbearable as
the dog leaned against him and licked his hand and, with
tail wagging, looked up at him with eyes that asked only

for friendship. "You're my—" the boy began again, but it was of no use to say it! He couldn't possibly keep the dog. The only thing to do was to take him up to Ed's Place and give him to the man who owned him. . . . "Come, boy," he said at last in a choking voice.

The wind was not blowing so hard now, but there was still that queer restless feeling in the air, and the smell of the sea and the darkening marshes was stronger than ever. With the dog beside him, friendly and trusting, Michael set off again toward the rolling pasture land. . . .

The light from the windows of the small restaurant cast squares of pale gold on the sandy road. At the door, Michael peered inside. At first he didn't see anyone. Then at the far end of the room he spied Ed seated at a little round table, talking with a man who wore a gray felt hat. In his hands resting on the table the man held something long and curved. As Michael recognized what it was he wanted to turn and go running back along the road. This man, he was certain, was the dog's owner, and the thing in his hands was a length of heavy braided leather, one end of which could be fastened to a dog's collar, the other end to be used, if needed, as a whip.

"Come," Michael said in an unsteady voice and, pushing the door open, stepped inside.

At sight of the boy and the huge dog, the two men rose quickly to their feet. Ed strode behind the counter, his eyes wide and round. The other, a tall man, came slowly forward. "Well!" he exclaimed. "Here's my dog! Where'd ye find him?"

"On the beach, sir," Michael began. "I was in the boat and—"

"What's that in yer hand?" the man interrupted him. Then as the boy drew the piece of chain all the way from his pocket, he added, "Well, what do ye know! Here's the rest of his collar I lost in the sand!" He took the piece of chain from Michael and, drawing the other half from his pocket, fitted the two together. One of the links had spread open, causing the collar to break; he closed the link by pressing it under his heel. "Here now," he said to the dog, "this time I want you to hold still and no nonsense!"

The dog laid back his ears and jerked his head sidewise.

As the man fingered the heavy end of the leather thong, Michael said quickly, "Come, boy, you'd better let him put the collar on you."

The dog wagged his tail and turned his head. Thereupon the man snapped the collar around his neck and fastened the thong to it. "Come along," he said, and took a step toward the door.

The dog refused to move.

"Come along!" The man jerked the thong.

Still the dog refused to move.

Michael moistened his lips. When he spoke he hardly recognized his voice, it was so hoarse and shaky. "Go with him, boy," he said. "Good—good-bye now!"

Dropping to his haunches, the dog playfully raised a forepaw.

Ed laughed and called from behind the counter, "Mister, I'd say he likes the boy better'n he likes you!"

The man frowned and jerked the thong again. As the dog refused to move, he said to Michael, "Get away from him! If you don't, I'll have to use the whip!"

"Please don't hit him!" Michael said and backed away.

"Now!" the man exclaimed and seized the metal collar.

The dog allowed himself to be pulled halfway to the door, but there he halted and swung his head toward Michael, nostrils sniffing, eyes alert and hopeful.

"Go along like a nice dog," Michael called.

Instead, as if loving the sound of the boy's voice, the dog jerked loose and returned to the middle of the floor. The man strode after him and grasped the thong.

"Oh, please don't hit him!" Michael said again. "Because if—"

"You keep quiet!" The man raised his voice angrily. "Get over there behind the counter—out of sight! You're the cause of the whole trouble!" And he took a step toward the boy.

Then a frightening thing happened. With a savage growl, the dog rushed at him, and in his fear and haste to get out of the way, the man overturned one of the tables. The next instant, hatless and wide-eyed, he was flat against the wall, the great dog on his hind legs holding him there, his bared gleaming teeth close to the man's white, terrified face.

"Get down!" Ed yelled, but the dog remained with forepaws against the man's chest, softly growling.

"Get down, boy!" Michael called and hurried toward them. "Don't hurt him!"

The dog stopped growling.

"Come now," Michael said quietly and put a hand on the gray bristling back. "Please, get down now! There, that's right."

As the dog dropped to all fours, the man drew a trembling hand across his mouth and began to edge cautiously toward the door, his eyes still wide and frightened.

"Hey, mister?" Ed called to him. "Not goin' away without yer dog, are ye?"

"I—I don't want a dog like that!" the man muttered—and hearing the words, Michael felt his heart leap!

"Oh, ye don't want him, eh?" Ed remarked, coming out from behind the counter. "Well, you want this, don't ye?" And picking up the gray felt hat, he crossed the floor with it. As the man set it nervously on his head, Ed added, "Mister, you never owned this dog in the first place, did ye?"

The man shook his head and moved nearer the door.

"Well, who owns him, then?" Ed asked—but the man had already slipped out the door and vanished into the twilight.

Ed turned to Michael. "Just as I suspected! The fellow prob'ly found this fine young wolfhound on the beach and—"

But Michael wasn't listening. The dog wasn't his, after all! Somebody owned him. "I'll take him home now," the boy said to himself unhappily, "but I know I can't keep him! Daddy will learn who the owner is and then—"

"What's the matter, boy?" Ed asked. "Ain't ye happy? You've got yer dog—"

"Oh, Ed, I can't keep him!" Michael cried. "He's valuable, and somebody's sure to claim him!"

Ed's eyes were kind. "You love him, don't you?"

Michael nodded, unable to speak.

"And the dog loves you," Ed added. "That's why he

pinned the fellow to the wall, because he thought he meant to harm ye! Whew, scared the daylights out of him!"

Michael removed the collar and placed it with the thong on one of the chairs. "Good-bye, Ed," he said and, with a hand on the dog's head, made his way to the door. . . .

In the west the first stars were faintly shining, and to the east stretched the dark ocean and the wide, dark marshes. Michael walked in silence along the soft road, and once more his throat was tight and his eyes ached. "If only I could tell Mom and Daddy this is my dog!" he said to himself.

He wondered who the owner might be and where he lived. Then raising his head hopefully, he murmured, "Maybe the owner lives near here and will let me come and see the dog once in a while!"

Halting abruptly, the boy looked back at Ed's Place, remembering that Ed always kept newspapers in a pile behind the counter. Maybe in one of those papers there would be a notice: "Lost—a valuable young Irish wolf-hound. . . ." And maybe it would tell who the owner was and where he lived!

Michael turned and set off back along the road. . . .

Ed was waiting on a customer when the boy and the dog appeared at the door. "Hi," he called. "Did ye forget somethin'? The dog collar and—"

Michael shook his head and pushed the door open. He didn't want the collar or the thong, either. He said, "I'd like to look at your newspapers. May I? Because there might be something about a lost dog—"

"That's right," Ed said. "Look on page two, under 'Lost and Found.'"

Michael carried half a dozen of the latest papers to one of the vacant tables and, while the dog lay on the floor close by, began eagerly to look through them. Under "Lost and Found" in the first newspaper there was nothing at all about a dog. Nor could he find anything in the second or the third or the fourth. He picked up the fifth and then the sixth, but, again, there was nothing about a dog.

Michael shook his head in disappointment. While he was making a neat pile of the papers, Ed called from across the room, "Find anything?"

"No—" Michael began and paused abruptly. Here on the back page of the latest paper was something about a dog! He bent quickly forward and read the headline: "Dog Leaps from Ship."

Michael's hands suddenly began to tremble as he read the fine print. It told about a big hunting dog that had belonged to a British sailor who had died in America just before his ship sailed. One of his mates took charge of the animal, but it was unhappy without its master and, when the vessel was on its way back to England, had leaped overboard and swum ashore. The account went on to describe the dog. . . .

"Well, boy, you've found somethin', haven't ye?" And there was Ed beside the table.

Michael handed him the paper, and Ed read the story.

"Maybe it's this dog!" Michael said breathlessly. "It could be, couldn't it, Ed? Oh, if only—"

"Hm," Ed said. "Big hunting dog, that's right. Short hair, smoky gray—that's right, too. Young dog, there again it's right. If you could be sure it's the same one, then he'd be yours, but unfortunately there must be other dogs like this one in the paper."

Michael nodded and was silent. Picking up the newspapers, he carried them back behind the counter. He didn't feel like looking at the other papers there. . . .

"Don't feel too bad over it," Ed said as the boy and the dog made their way to the door again.

Michael managed a smile; but once more on the road, his hand caressing one of the dog's pointed ears, he walked with dragging steps, his eyes staring unhappily into the darkness. It was growing late, and he knew his mother and father would be worried about him, but his disappointment was so deep he could think of almost nothing else. . . .

He was more than halfway home when once again he halted abruptly, recalling the very last sentence in the newspaper story: "The dog's name is—" Michael swallowed excitedly and looked quickly downward at his companion stretched out in the soft sand. "Why didn't I think of it before?" the boy exclaimed. Here was a simple way of learning whether this was the same dog that had leaped from the ship!

Michael opened his mouth, then closed it, suddenly afraid to make the test. Yet he must make it! He must find out!

Walking to the far side of the road, he seated himself among tall meadow grasses. The dog lifted his head and looked at him, then, seeing that the boy was just sitting there, let his head fall again. "He's awfully tired," Michael thought. He himself was excited and worried. Supposing the test should prove that the dog was not the one that had leaped from the ship? Supposing . . .

As a puff of cool air from the sea fanned his face, Michael looked up at the brightening stars. Then he looked again at the sleeping dog.

"Hi, Smoky?" he said.

The dog merely stretched his legs far out and made a faint grunting sound.

Michael waited perhaps a full minute. Then he said, "Hi, Rover?"

The dog hardly moved.

Michael took a deep breath while his heart began to pound. Now was the moment! But he mustn't show how eager and excited he was. . . .

Quietly—even more quietly than he had spoken the other two names—he said, "Hi, Kildare?"

The effect was so sudden he caught his breath! Amid a wild scurry of sand the dog uttered a surprised yelp and, leaping to his feet, came bounding across the road. Before Michael could move, the huge creature was all over him, licking at his face and barking joyfully. . . .

"Hey, let me up!" the boy protested at last, and squirming sidewise he managed to push himself to his feet. Then, "Kildare!" he repeated triumphantly and threw his arms around the dog's neck, again recalling the last sentence in the news story: "The dog's name is Kildare."

The test had worked the way he hoped it would! He

could have no doubt now that this was the same dog that had leaped from the ship.

"Kildare—Oh, Kildare, you're my dog!" he exclaimed happily—and this time it was true!

Together, like old friends, the two of them set off homeward while overhead the stars grew brighter and brighter.

The Comet

by Samuel A. Derieux

NO PUPPY EVER CAME into the world under more favorable conditions than Comet. He was descended from a famous family of pointers. Both his mother and father were champions. Before he opened his eyes, while he was still crawling about over his brother and sisters, blind as puppies are at birth, Jim Thompson, Mr. Devant's kennel master, picked him out:

"That's the best 'un in the bunch."

When he was only three weeks old, he pointed a butterfly that lit in the yard in front of his nose.

"Come here, Molly," yelled Jim to his wife. "Pointed— the little cuss!"

When Thompson started taking the growing pups out of the yard, into the fields to the side of Devant's great southern winter home, Oak Knob, it was Comet who strayed farthest from the man's protecting care. And when Jim taught them all to follow when he said "Heel," to drop when he said "Drop," and to stand stock-still when he said "Ho," he learned far more quickly than the others.

At six months he set his first covey of quail, and remained perfectly stanch. "He's goin' to make a great dog," said Thompson. Everything—size, muscle, nose, intelligence, earnestness—pointed to the same conclusion. Comet was one of the favored of the gods.

One day, after the leaves had turned red and brown and the mornings grown chilly, a crowd of people, strangers to him, arrived at Oak Knob. Then out of the house with Thompson came a big man in tweed clothes, and the two walked straight to the curious young dogs, who were watching them with shining eyes and wagging tails.

"Well, Thompson," said the big man. "Which is the future champion you've been writing me about?"

"Pick him out for yourself, sir," said Thompson confidently.

After that they talked a long time planning for the future of Comet. His yard training was now over (Thompson was only yard trainer), and he must be sent to a man experienced in training and handling for field trials.

"Larsen's the man to bring him out," said the big man in tweeds, who was George Devant himself. "I saw his dogs work in the Canadian Derby."

Thompson spoke hesitatingly, apologetically, as if he hated to bring the matter up. "Mr. Devant . . . you remember, sir, a long time ago Larsen sued us for old Ben."

"Yes, Thompson, I remember, now that you speak of it."

"Well, you remember the court decided against him, which was the only thing it could do, for Larsen didn't have any more right to that dog than the sultan of Turkey. But, Mr. Devant, I was there, and I saw Larsen's face when the case went against him."

Devant looked keenly at Thompson.

"Another thing, Mr. Devant," Thompson went on, still hesitatingly, "Larsen had a chance to get hold of this breed of pointers and lost out, because he dickered too long, and acted cheesy. Now they've turned out to be famous. Some men never forget a thing like that. Larsen's been talkin' these pointers down ever since, sir."

"Go on," said Devant.

"I know Larsen's a good trainer. But it'll mean a long trip for the young dog to where he lives. Now, there's an old trainer lives near here, Wade Swygert. There never was a straighter man than him. He used to train dogs in England."

Devant smiled. "Thompson, I admire your loyalty to your friends; but I don't think much of your business sense. We'll turn over some of the others to Swygert, if he wants 'em. Comet must have the best. I'll write Larsen tonight, Thompson. Tomorrow, crate Comet and send him off."

Just as no dog ever came into the world under more favorable auspices, so no dog ever had a bigger send-off than Comet. Even the ladies of the house came out to exclaim over him, and Marian Devant, pretty, eighteen, and a sportswoman, stooped down, caught his head between her hands, looked into his fine eyes and wished him "Good luck, old man." In the living room the men laughingly drank toasts to his future, and from the high-columned portico Marian Devant waved him good-by, as in his clean, padded crate he was driven off, a bewildered youngster, to the station.

Two days and two night he traveled, and at noon of the third day, at a lonely railroad station in a prairie country that rolled like a heavy sea, he was lifted, crate and all, off the train. A lean, pale-eyed, sanctimonious-looking man came toward him.

"Some beauty that, Mr. Larsen," said the agent as he helped Larsen's man lift the crate onto a small truck.

"Yes," drawled Larsen in a meditative voice, "pretty enough to look at, but he looks scared—er—timid."

"Of course he's scared," said the agent. "So would you be if they was to put you in some kind of a whale of a balloon an' ship you in a crate to Mars."

The station agent poked his hands through the slats and patted the head. Comet was grateful for that, because everything was strange. He had not whined or complained on the trip, but his heart had pounded fast, and he had been homesick.

And everything had continued to be strange: the treeless country through which he was driven, the bald house, the huge barns where he was lifted out, the dogs that crowded about him when he was turned into the kennel yard. These eyed him with enmity and walked round and round him. But he stood his ground stanchly for a youngster, returning fierce look for fierce look, growl for growl, until the man called him away and chained him to a kennel.

For days Comet remained chained, a stranger in a strange land. Each time at the click of the gate announcing Larsen's entrance, he sprang to his feet from force of habit, and stared hungrily at the man for the light he was accustomed to see in human eyes. But with just a glance at him, the man would turn one or more of the other dogs loose and ride off to train them.

But he was not without friends of his own kind. Now and then another young dog (he alone was chained up) would stroll his way with wagging tail, or lie down nearby, in that strange bond of sympathy that is not confined to man. Then Comet would feel better and would want to play, for he was still half puppy. Sometimes he would pick up a stick and shake it, and his partner would catch the other end. They would tug and growl with mock ferocity, and then lie down and look at each other curiously.

If any attention had been paid him by Larsen, Comet would have quickly overcome his feeling of strangeness. He was no milksop. He was like an overgrown boy, off at college, or in some foreign city. He was sensitive, and not sure of himself. Had Larsen gained his confidence, it would all have been different. And as for Larsen—he knew that perfectly well.

One fine sunny afternoon, Larsen entered the yard, came straight to him, and turned him loose. In the exuberance of his spirits he ran around and around the yard, barking in the faces of his friends. Larsen let him out, mounted a horse and commanded him to heel. He obeyed with wagging tail.

A mile or more down the road, Larsen turned off into the fields. Across his saddle was something the young pointer had had no experience with—a gun. That part of his education Thompson had neglected, at least put off, for he had not expected that Comet would be sent away so soon. That was where Thompson had made a mistake.

At the command "Hi on" the young pointer ran eagerly around the horse, and looked up into the man's face to be sure he had heard aright. At something he saw there, the tail and ears drooped momentarily, and there came over him again a feeling of strangeness, almost of dismay. Larsen's eyes were mere slits of blue glass, and his mouth was set in a thin line.

At a second command, though, he galloped off swiftly, boldly. Around and around an extensive field of straw he circled, forgetting any feeling of strangeness now, every fiber of his being intent on the hunt, while Larsen, sitting on his horse, watched him with appraising eyes.

Suddenly there came to Comet's nose the smell of game birds, strong, pungent, compelling. He stiffened into an earnest, beautiful point. Heretofore in the little training he had had, Thompson had come up behind him, flushed the birds, and made him drop. And now Larsen, having quickly dismounted and tied his horse, came up behind him, just as Thompson had done, except that in Larsen's hand was the gun.

The old-fashioned black powder of a generation ago makes a loud explosion. It sounds like a cannon, compared with the modern smokeless powder now used by all hunters. Perhaps it was only an accident that had caused Larsen before he left the house to load his pump gun with black-powder shells.

As for Comet, he only knew that the birds rose; then above his head burst an awful roar, almost splitting his tender eardrums, shocking every sensitive nerve, filling him with terror such as he had never felt before. Even then, in the confusion and horror of the surprise, he turned to the man, head ringing, eyes dilated. A single reassuring word, and he would have steadied. As for Larsen, though, he declared afterward (to others and to himself even) that he noticed no nervousness in the dog; that he was only intent on getting several birds for breakfast.

Twice, three times, four times, the pump gun bellowed in its cannon-like roar, piercing the eardrums, shattering the nerves. Comet turned; one more glance backward at a face, strange, exultant—and then the puppy in him conquered. Tail tucked, he ran away from that shattering noise.

Miles he ran. Now and then, stumbling over briars, he yelped. Not once did he look back. His tail was tucked, his eyes crazy with fear. Seeing a house, he made for that. It was the noon hour and a group of farm hands was gathered in the yard. One of them, with a cry, "Mad dog," ran into the house after a gun. When he came out, they told him the dog was under the porch. And so he was. Pressed against the wall, in the darkness, the magnificent young pointer with the quivering soul waited, panting, eyes gleaming, the horror still ringing in his ears.

Here Larsen found him that afternoon. A boy crawled underneath the porch and dragged him out. He, who had started life favored of the gods, who that morning even had been full of high spirits, who had circled a field like a champion, was now a cringing, shaking creature, like a homeless cur.

And thus it happened that Comet came home, in disgrace—a gun-shy dog, a coward, expelled from college, not for some youthful prank, but because he was—yellow. And he knew he was disgraced. He saw it in the face of the big man, Devant, who looked at him in the yard where he had spent his happy puppyhood, then turned away. He knew it because of what he saw in the face of Jim Thompson.

In the house was a long and plausible letter, explaining how it had happened:

I did everything I could. I never was as surprised in my life. The dog's hopeless.

As for the other inhabitants of the big house, their minds were full of the events of the season: deluxe hunting parties, more society events than hunts; lunches in the woods served by uniformed butlers, launch rides up the river, arriving and departing guests. Only one of them, except Devant himself, gave the gun-shy dog a thought. Marian Devant came out to visit him in his disgrace. She stooped before him as she had done on that other and happier day, and again caught his head between her hands. But his eyes did not meet hers, for in his dim way he knew he was not now what he had been.

"I don't believe he's yellow—inside!" she declared, looking up at Thompson, her cheeks flushed.

Thompson shook his head.

"I tried him with a gun, Miss Marian," he declared, "I just showed it to him, and he ran into his kennel."

"I'll go get mine. He won't run from me."

But at sight of her small gun it all came back. Again he seemed to hear the explosion that had shattered his nerves. The terror had entered his very soul. In spite of her pleading, he made for his kennel. Even the girl turned away from him now. And as he lay panting in the shelter of his kennel he knew that never again would men look at him as they had looked, or life be sweet to him as it had been.

Then there came to Oak Knob an old man, to see Thompson. He had been on many seas, he had fought in a dozen wars, and had settled at last on a little truck farm nearby. Somewhere, in his life full of adventure and odd jobs, he had trained dogs and horses. His face was lined and seamed, his hair was white, his eyes piercing, blue and kind. Wade Swygert was his name.

"There's been dirty work," he said, when he looked at the dog. "I'll take him if you're goin' to give him away."

Give him away—who had been championship hope!

Marian Devant came out and looked into the face of the old man, shrewdly, understandingly.

"Can you cure him?" she demanded.

"I doubt it, miss," was the sturdy answer.

"You will try?"

The blue eyes lighted up. "Yes, I'll try."

"Then you can have him. And—if there's any expense—"

"Come, Comet," said the old man.

That night, in a neat, humble house, Comet ate supper placed before him by a stout old woman, who had followed this old man to the ends of the world. That night he slept before their fire. Next day he followed the old man all about the place. Several days and nights passed this way, then, while he lay before the fire, old Swygert

came in with a gun. At sight of it, Comet sprang to his feet. He tried to rush out of the room, but the doors were closed. Finally, he crawled under the bed.

Every night after that Swygert got out the gun, until he crawled under the bed no more. Finally, one day the man fastened the dog to a tree in the yard, then came out with a gun. A sparrow lit in a tree, and he shot it. Comet tried to break the rope. All his panic had returned; but the report had not shattered him as that other did, for the gun was loaded light.

After that, frequently the old man shot a bird in his sight, loading the gun more and more heavily, and each time after the shot, coming to him, showing him the bird, and speaking to him kindly, gently. But for all that, the terror remained in his heart.

One afternoon the girl, accompanied by a young man,

rode over on horseback, dismounted and came in. She always stopped when she was riding by.

"It's mighty slow business," old Swygert reported. "I don't know whether I'm makin' any headway or not."

That night old Mrs. Swygert told him she thought he had better give it up. It wasn't worth the time and worry. The dog was just yellow.

Swygert pondered a long time. "When I was a kid," he said at last, "there came up a terrible thunderstorm. It was in South America. I was water boy for a railroad gang, and the storm drove us in a shack. While lightnin' was hittin' all around, one of the grown men told me it always picked out boys with red hair. My hair was red, an' I was little and ignorant. For years I was skeered of lightnin'. I never have quite got over it. But no man ever said I was yellow."

Again he was silent for a while. Then he went on: "I don't seem to be makin' much headway, I admit that. I'm lettin' him run away as far as he can. Now I've got to shoot an' make him come toward the gun himself, right while I'm shootin' it."

Next day Comet was tied up and fasted, and next, until he was gaunt and famished. Then, on the afternoon of the third day, Mrs. Swygert, at her husband's direction, placed before him, within reach of his chain, some raw beefsteak. As he started for it, Swygert shot. He drew back, panting; then, hunger getting the better of him, started again. Again Swygert shot.

After that for days Comet "ate to music," as Swygert expressed it. "Now," he said, "he's got to come toward the gun when he's not even tied up."

Not far from Swygert's house is a small pond, and on one side the banks are perpendicular. Toward this pond the old man, with the gun under his arm and the dog following, went. Here in the silence of the woods, with just the two of them together, was to be a final test.

On the shelving bank Swygert picked up a stick and tossed it into the middle of the pond with the command, "Fetch." Comet sprang eagerly in and retrieved it. Twice this was repeated. But the third time, as the dog approached the shore, Swygert picked up the gun and fired.

Quickly the dog dropped the stick, then turned and swam to the other shore. Here, so precipitous were the banks, he could not get a foothold. He turned once more and struck out diagonally across the pond. Swygert met him and fired.

Over and over it happened. Each time, after he fired, the old man stooped down with extended hand and begged him to come on. His face was grim now and, though the day was cool, sweat stood out on his brow. "You'll face the music," he said, "or you'll drown. Better be dead than called yellow."

The dog was growing weary now. His head was barely above water. His efforts to clamber up the opposite bank were feeble, frantic. Yet, each time as he drew near the shore Swygert fired.

He was not using light loads now. He was using the regular load of the bird hunter. Time had passed for temporizing. The sweat was standing out all over his face. The sternness in his eyes was terrible to see, for it was the sternness of a man who is suffering.

A dog can swim a long time. The sun dropped over the trees. Still the firing went on, regularly, like a minute gun.

Just before the sun set an exhausted dog staggered toward an old man, almost as exhausted as he. The dog had been too near death and was too faint to care now for the gun that was being fired over his head. On and on he came, toward the man, disregarding the noise of the gun. It would not hurt him, that he knew at last. He might have many enemies, but the gun, in the hands of this man, was not one of them. Suddenly old Swygert sank down and took the dripping dog in his arms.

"Old boy," he said, "old boy."

That night Comet lay before the fire, and looked straight into the eyes of a man, as he used to look in the old days.

Next season, Larsen, glancing over his sporting papers, was astonished to see that among promising derbies the fall trials had called forth was a pointer named Comet. He would have thought it some other dog than the one who had disappointed him so by turning out gun-shy, in spite of all his efforts to prevent it, had it not been for the fact that the entry was booked as "Comet; owner, Miss Marian Devant; handler, Wade Swygert."

Next year he was still more astonished to see in the same paper that Comet, handled by Swygert, had won first place in a Western trial, and was prominently spoken of as a National Championship possibility. As for him, he had no young entries to offer, but was staking everything on the National Championship, where he was to enter Larsen's Peerless II.

It was strange how things fell out—but things have a habit of turning out strangely in field trials, as well as elsewhere. When Larsen reached the town where the National Championship was to be run, there on the street, straining at the leash held by old Swygert, whom he used to know, was a seasoned young pointer, with a white body, a brown head and a brown saddle spot—the same pointer he had seen two years before turn tail and run in that terror a dog never quite overcomes.

It gave Larsen a strange thrill. He left the meeting and went straightway to his room. There for a long time he sat pondering. Next day at a hardware store he bought some black powder, and some shells.

The race was to be run next day, and that night in his room he loaded half a dozen shells. It would have been a study in faces to watch him as he bent over his work, on his lips a smile. Into the shells he packed all the powder they could stand, all the powder his trusted gun could stand, without bursting. It was a load big enough to kill a bear, to bring down a buffalo. It was a load that would echo and re-echo in the hills.

On the morning that Larsen walked out in front of the judges and the field, Peerless II at the leash, old Swygert with Comet at his side, he glanced around at the "field," or spectators. Among them was a handsome young woman, and with her, to his amazement, George Devant. He could not help chuckling inside himself as he thought of what would happen that day, for once a gun-shy dog, always a gun-shy dog—that was *his* experience.

As for Comet, he faced the straw fields eagerly, confidently, already a veteran. Long ago fear of the gun had left him, for the most part. There were times, when at a report above his head, he still trembled, and the shocked nerves in his ear gave a twinge like that of a bad tooth. But always at the quiet voice of the old man, his god, he grew steady, and remained stanch.

Some disturbing memory did start within him today as he glanced at the man with the other dog. It seemed to him as if in another and an evil world he had seen that face. His heart began to pound fast, and his tail drooped for a moment. Within an hour it was all to come back to him—the terror, the panic, the agony of that faraway time.

He looked up at old Swygert, who was his god, and to whom his soul belonged, though he was booked as the property of Miss Marian Devant. Of the arrangements he could know nothing, being a dog. Old Swygert, having cured him, could not meet the expenses of taking him to field trials. The girl had come to the old man's assistance, an assistance which he had accepted only under condition that the dog should be entered as hers, with himself as handler.

"Are you ready, gentlemen?" the judges asked.

"Ready," said Larsen and old Swygert.

And Comet and Peerless II were speeding away across that field, and behind them came handlers, and judges and spectators, all mounted.

It was a race people still talk about, and for a reason, for strange things happened that day. At first there was nothing unusual. It was like any other field trial. Comet found birds, and Swygert, his handler, flushed them and shot. Comet remained steady. Then Peerless II found a covey, and Larsen flushed them and shot. And so for an hour it went.

Then Comet disappeared, and old Swygert, riding hard and looking for him, went out of sight over a hill. But Comet had not gone far. As a matter of fact he was nearby, hidden in some high straw, pointing a covey of birds. One of the spectators spied him, and called the judges' attention to him. Everybody, including Larsen, rode up to him, but still Swygert had not come back.

They called him, but the old man was a little deaf. Some of the men rode to the top of the hill, but could not see him. In his zeal, he had got a considerable distance away. Meanwhile, here was his dog, pointed.

If anyone had looked at Larsen's face he would have seen the exultation there, for now his chance had come —the very chance he had been looking for. It's a courtesy one handler sometimes extends another who is absent from the spot, to go in and flush his dog's birds.

"I'll handle this covey for Mr. Swygert," said Larsen to the judges, his voice smooth and plausible, on his face a smile.

And thus it happened that Comet faced his supreme ordeal without the steadying voice of his god.

He only knew that ahead of him were birds, and that behind him a man was coming through the straw, and that behind the man a crowd of people on horseback were watching him. He had become used to that, but when, out of the corner of his eye, he saw the face of the advancing man, his soul began to tremble.

"Call your dog in, Mr. Larsen," directed the judge. "Make him backstand."

Only a moment was lost, while Peerless II, a young dog himself, came running in and at a command from Larsen stopped in his tracks behind Comet, and pointed. Larsen's dogs always obeyed, quickly, mechanically. Without ever gaining their confidence, Larsen had a way of turning them into finished field-trial dogs. They obeyed, because they were afraid not to.

According to the rules the man handling the dog has to shoot as the birds rise. This is done in order to test the dog's steadiness when a gun is fired over him. No specification is made as to the size of the shotgun to be used. Usually, however, small-gauge guns are carried. The one in Larsen's hands was a twelve gauge, and consequently large.

All morning he had been using it over his own dog. Nobody had paid any attention to it, because he shot smokeless powder. But now, as he advanced, he reached into the left-hand pocket of his hunting coat, where six shells rattled as he hurried along. Two of these he took out and rammed into the barrels.

As for Comet, still standing rigid, statuesque, he heard, as has been said, the brush of steps through the straw, glimpsed a face, and trembled. But only for a moment. Then he steadied, head high, tail straight out. The birds rose with a whir—and then was repeated that horror of his youth. Above his ears, ears that would always be tender, broke a great roar. Either because of his excitement, or because of a sudden wave of revenge, or of a determination to make sure of the dog's flight, Larsen pulled both triggers at once. The combined report shattered through the dog's eardrums, it shivered through his nerves; he sank in agony into the straw.

Then the old impulse to flee was upon him, and he sprang to his feet, and looked about wildly. But from somewhere in that crowd behind him came to his tingling ears a voice—clear, ringing, deep, the voice of a woman —a woman he knew—pleading as his master used to plead, calling on him not to run, but to stand.

"Steady," it said. "Steady, Comet!"

It called him to himself, it soothed him, it calmed him, and he turned and looked toward the crowd. With the roar of the shotgun the usual order observed in field trials was broken up. All rules seemed to have been suspended. Ordinarily no one belonging to the "field" is allowed to speak to a dog. Yet the girl had spoken to him. Ordinarily, the spectators must remain in the rear of the judges. Yet one of the judges had himself wheeled his horse about and was galloping off, and Marian Devant had pushed through the crowd and was riding toward the bewildered dog.

He stood staunch where he was, though in his ears was still a throbbing pain, and though all about him was this growing confusion he could not understand. The man he feared was running across the field yonder, in the direction taken by the judge. He was blowing his whistle as he ran. Through the crowd, his face terrible to see, his own master was coming. Both the old man and the girl had dismounted now, and were running toward him.

"I heard," old Swygert was saying to her. "I heard it! I might 'a' known! I might 'a' known!"

"He stood," she panted, "like a rock—oh, the brave, beautiful thing!"

"Where is that—" Swygert suddenly checked himself and looked around.

A man in the crowd (they had all gathered about now) laughed.

"He's gone after his dog," he said. "Peerless has run away!"

The Coward

by *Albert Payson Terhune*

IT BEGAN WHEN LAUND was a rangily gawky six-month puppy and when Danny Crae was only seven years old. Danny had claimed the spraddling little fluffball of a collie as his own on the day the boy's father lifted the two-month-old puppy out of the yard where Laund lived and played and slept and had a wonderful time with his several brothers and sisters.

On that morning Ronald Crae ordained that the brown-and-white baby collie was to become a herder of sheep and a guard of the house and farm. On that morning seven-year-old Danny announced that Laund was to be his very own dog and help him herd his adored bantams.

Now, Ronald Crae was not given to knuckling under to anyone. But he had a strangely gentle way with him as concerned this crippled son of his. Therefore, instead of the sharp rebuke Danny had a right to expect for putting his own wishes against his sire's, Ronald petted the wan little face and told Danny jokingly that they would share

186

Laund in partnership. Part of the time the puppy should herd the Crae sheep and do other farm work. Part of the time he should be Danny's playfellow. And so it was arranged.

A year earlier, a fearsome pestilence had scourged America, sending black horror to the heart of ten million mothers throughout the land and claiming thousands of little children as its victims. Danny Crae had been but brushed lightly by the hem of the pestilence's robe. He did not die, as did so many children in his own township. But he rose from a three-month illness with useless legs that would not move nor bear a fraction of his frail weight.

Quickly he learned to make his way around, after a fashion, by means of double crutches. But every doctor declared he must be a hopeless and half-helpless cripple for life.

Small wonder his usually dominant father did not veto any plan of his stricken child's! Small wonder he skimped the hours of herd-training for Laund, in order to leave the puppy free to be the playmate of the sick boy!

In spite of this handicap, young Laund picked up the rudiments and then the finer points of his herding work with an almost bewildering swiftness and accuracy. Ronald Crae was an excellent trainer, to be sure; firm and self-controlled and commonsensible, if a trifle stern with his dogs; and a born dogman. But the bulk of the credit went to the puppy himself. He was one of those not wholly rare collies that pick up their work as though they had known it all before and were remembering rather than learning.

Crae was proud of the little dog. Presently he began to plan entering him sometime in the yearly field trials of the National Collie Association, confident that Laund would be nearer the front than the rear of that stiff competition.

Then, when the puppy was six months old, Crae changed his opinion of the promising youngster—changed it sharply and disgustedly. It happened in this wise:

Of old, Danny had rejoiced to go afield with his father and to watch the rounding up and driving and folding and penning of the farm's sheep. Now that he was able to move only a little way and on slow crutches, the child transferred his attention to a flock of pedigreed bantams his father had bought him and which were the boy's chief delight.

Like Ronald, he had a way with dumb things. The tame bantams let him handle them at will. They ate from his wizened fingers and lighted on his meagerly narrow and uneven shoulders for food. Then it occurred to him to teach Laund to herd and drive them. Luckily for his plan and for the safety and continued tameness of the little flock of chickens, Laund was as gentle with them as with the youngest of his master's lambs. Gravely and tenderly he would herd them, at Danny's shrill order, avoiding stepping on any of them or frightening them.

It was a pretty sight. Watching it, and Danny's delight in the simple maneuvers, Ronald forgot his own annoyance in having to share a valuable puppy's valuable training time with his son.

One day Danny and Laund sat side by side on a rock, back of the barnyard, watching the bantams scramble for handfuls of thrown feed. Among the flock was a tiny mother hen with a half dozen downily diminutive chicks. Anxiously she clucked to them as she grabbed morsel after morsel of the feast, and tried to shove the other bantams aside to give place to her babies where the feed was thickest.

As the last of the flung grain was gobbled, the flock dispersed. Most of them drifted to the barnyard. The mother hen and her chicks strayed out toward the truck garden, some fifty feet in front of where the boy and the dog were sitting.

Of a sudden the tiny mother crouched, with a raucously crooning cry to her children, spreading her wings for them to hide under. As they ran to her, a dark shadow swept the sunlit earth. Down from nowhere a huge hen hawk shot, like a brown feathery cannon ball, diving at the baby bantams and at their frightened dam.

"Laund!" squealed Danny, pointing to the chicks.

The six-month puppy leaped to them. He had no idea why he was sent thither or what he was supposed to do. He did not see the swooping hawk. Never had he even seen a hawk before, though hawks were plentiful enough in that mountain region. But he noted the flustered excitement of the hen and the scurrying of the golden mites toward her and the alarm in Danny's loved voice. Wherefore he bounded alertly into the arena—to do he knew not what.

As a matter of fact, there was nothing for him to do.

As he reached the hen, something dark and terrible clove its way downward, so close to him that the air of it fanned his ruff.

A chick was seized and the hawk beat its way upward.

Instinctively, Laund sprang at the bird, before its mighty pinions could lift it clear of the earth. He leaped upon it right valorously and dug his half-developed teeth into its shoulder.

Then, all the skies seemed to be falling, and smiting Laund as they fell.

A handful of feathers came away in his mouth, as the hawk dropped the mangled chick and wheeled about on the half-grown puppy that had pinched its shoulder.

The drivingly powerful wings lambasted him with fearful force and precision, knocking him off his feet, beating the breath out of him, half-blinding him. The hooked beak drove a knife-gash along his side. The talons sank momentarily, but deep, into the tender flesh of his underbody.

It was not a fight. It was a massacre. Laund had not time to collect his faculties nor even to note clearly what manner of monster this was. All he knew was that a creature had swept down from the sky, preceded by a blotty black shadow, and was well-nigh murdering him.

In a second it was over. Even as Danny yelled to the bird and as he gathered his crutches under him to struggle to his feet, the giant hawk had lurched away from the screeching and rolling puppy; had snatched up the dead chick, and was beating its way skyward.

That was all. On the recently placid sunlit sward below, a frantically squawking hen ran to and fro amid five piping and scurrying chicks; and a brown collie wallowed about, waking the echoes with his terror yelps.

In all his six months of life Laund had known no cruelty, no pain, no ill-treatment. He had learned to herd sheep, as a pastime to himself. He had not dreamed there could be agony and danger in the fulfilling of any of his farm duties.

Now, while still he was scarcely more than a baby—while his milk teeth were still shedding, before his collie character could knit to courage and tense fortitude—he had been frightened out of his young wits and had been cruelly hurt and battered about; all by this mysterious and shadow-casting monster from the sky.

Through his howling he was peering upward in shuddering dread at the slowly receding giant hawk. Its blackness against the sun, its sinister sweep of pinion, its soaring motion, all stamped themselves indelibly on the puppy's shocked brain. More—the taste of its feathers was in his mouth. Its rank scent was strong in his nostrils. Dogs record impressions by odor even more than by sight. That hawk reek was never to leave Laund's memory.

The pup's wails, and Danny's, brought the household thither on the run. Laund was soothed and his hurts and bruises were tended, while Danny's own excitement was gently calmed. The doctors had said the little cripple must not be allowed to excite himself, and that any strong emotion was bad for his twisted nerves.

In a few days Laund was well again, his flesh wounds healing with the incredible quickness that goes with the perfect physical condition of a young outdoor collie. Apparently he was none the worse for his experience. Ronald Crae understood dogs well, and he had watched keenly to see if the pup's gay spirit was cowed by his mishandling from the hawk. As he could see no sign of this, he was genuinely relieved. A cowed dog makes a poor sheepherder and a worse herder of cattle.

Crae did not tell Danny what he had feared. If he had, the child would have given him a less optimistic slant on the case. For more than once Danny saw Laund wince and cower when a low-flying pigeon chanced to winnow just above him on its flight from cote to barnyard.

It was a week later that Laund was driving a bunch of skittish and silly wethers across the road from the home fold to the first sheep pasture. Outwardly it was a simple job. All that need be done was to get them safely through the fold gate and out into the yard; thence through the yard gate out into the road; thence across the road and in through the home-pasture gate which Ronald Crae was holding open.

It was one of the easiest of Laund's duties. True, there was always an off-chance of the wethers trying to scatter or of one of them bolting down the road instead of into the pasture.

But the young dog had an instinct for this sort of thing. Like the best of his ancestors, he seemed to read the sheep's minds—if indeed sheep are blest or cursed with minds—and to know beforehand in just what direction one or more of them were likely to break formation. Always he was on the spot; ready to turn back the galloping stray and to keep the rest from following the seceder.

Today, he marshaled the milling bunch as snappily and cleanly as ever, herding them across the yard and to the road. On these wethers he wasted none of the gentleness he lavished on heavy ewes or on lambs. This, too, was an ancestral throwback, shared by a thousand other sheep-driving collies.

Into the road debouched the baaing and jostling flock. As ever, they were agog for any chance to get into mischief. Indeed, they were more than usually ready for it. For their ears were assailed by an unwonted sound—a far-off whirring that made them nervous.

Laund heard the sound, too, and was mildly intrested in it; though it conveyed no meaning to him. Steadily he sent his wethers out into the road in a gray-white pattering cloud. Through the yard gate he dashed after them, on the heels of the hindmost; keyed up to the snappy task of making them cross the road without the compact bunch disintegrating; and on through the pasture gateway where Crae stood.

As his forefeet touched the edge of the road, a giant black shadow swept the yellow dust in front of him. The whirring waxed louder. Frightened, gripped by an unnameable terror, Laund glanced upward.

Above his head, sharply outlined against the pale blue of the sky, was a hawk a hundred times larger than the one that had assaulted him. Very near it seemed—very near and indescribably terrible.

A state forest ranger, scouting for signs of mountain fires, glanced down from his airplane at the pastoral scene below him—the pretty farmstead, the flock of sheep crossing the road, the alert brown collie dog marshaling them. Then the aeronaut was treated to another and more interesting sight.

Even as he looked, the faithful dog ceased from his task of sheep-driving. Ki-yi-ing in piercing loudness, and with furry tail clamped between his hindlegs and with stomach to earth, the dog deserted his post of duty and fled madly toward the refuge of the open kitchen door.

Infected by his screaming terror, the sheep scattered up and down the road, scampering at top speed in both directions and dashing anywhere except in through the gateway where Ronald Crae danced up and down in profane fury.

The plane whirred on into the distance, its amused pilot ignorant that he was the cause of the spectacular panic or that a fool puppy had mistaken his machine for a punitive henhawk.

After a long and angry search, Laund was found far under Danny's bed, huddled with his nose in a dusty corner and trembling all over.

"That settles it!" stormed Crae. "He's worthless. He's a cur—a mutt. He's yellow to the core. If it wasn't that Danny loves him so I'd waste an ounce of buckshot on him, here and now. It's the only way to treat a collie that is such an arrant coward. He—"

"But, dear," protested his wife, while Danny sobbed in mingled grief over his collie chum's disgrace and in shame that Laund should have proved so pusillanimous, "you said yourself that he is the best sheep dog for his age you've ever trained. Just because he ran away the first time he saw an airship it's no sign he won't be valuable to you in farm work. He—"

" 'No sign,' hey?" he growled. "Suppose he is working a bunch of sheep near a precipice or over a bridge that hasn't a solid side rail—suppose an airship happens to sail over him, or a hawk? There's plenty of both hereabouts, these days. What is due to happen? Or if he is on herd duty in the upper pasture and a hawk or an airship sends him scuttling to cover, a mile away, what's to prevent anyone from stealing a sheep or two? Or what's to prevent stray dogs from raiding them? Besides, a dog that is a coward is no dog to have around us. He's yellow. He's worthless. If it wasn't for Danny—"

He saw his son trying to fight back the tears and slipping a wasted little arm around the cowering Laund. With a grunt, Ronald broke off in his tirade and stamped away.

More than a month passed before he would so much as look at the wistfully friendly puppy again or let him handle the sheep.

With all a collie's high sensitiveness, Laund realized he was in disgrace. He knew it had something to do with his panic flight from the airship. To the depths of him he was ashamed. But to save his life he could not conquer that awful terror for soaring birds. It had become a part of him.

Wherefore, he turned unhappily to Danny for comfort, even though his instinct told him the boy no longer felt for him the admiring chumship of old days. Laund, Danny, Ronald—all, according to their natures—were wretched, in their own ways, because of the collie's shameful behavior.

Yet, even black disgrace wears its own sharpest edge dull, in time. Laund was the only dog left on the farm. He was imperatively needful for the herding. He was

Danny's only chum, and a chum was imperatively need-ful to Danny. Thus, bit by bit, Laund slipped back into his former dual position of herder and pal, even though Ronald had lost all faith in his courage in emergency.

A bit of this faith was revived when Laund was about fourteen months old. He was driving a score of ewes and spindly-legged baby lambs home to the fold from the lush South Mowing. There was a world of difference in his method of handling them from his whirlwind tactics with a bunch of wethers.

Slowly and with infinite pains he eased them along the short stretch of road between the pasture and the farm-stead; keeping the frisky lambs from galloping from their fellows by interposing his shaggy body between them and their way to escape, and softly edging them back to their mothers. The ewes he kept in formation by pushing his head gently against their flanks as they sought to stray or to lag.

Even Ronald Crae gave grudging approval to strong young Laund coaxing his willful charges to their destina-tion. Try as he would, the man could find nothing to criticize in the collie's work.

"There's not a dog that can hold a candle to him, in any line of shepherding," muttered Crae to himself as he plodded far behind the woolly band. "If he hadn't the heart of a rabbit there'd be every chance for him to clean up the Grand Prize at the National Collie Association field trials next month. But I was a fool to enter him for them, I suppose. A dog that'll turn tail and run to hide under a bed when he sees an airship or a hawk will never have the nerve to go through those stiff tests. He—"

Crae stopped short in his maundering thoughts. Laund had just slipped to the rear of the flock to cajole a tired ewe into rejoining the others. At the same moment a scatter-wit lambkin in the front rank gamboled far forward from the bunch.

A huge and hairy stray mongrel lurched out of a clump of wayside undergrowth and seized the stray lamb. Crae saw, and with a shout he ran forward.

But he was far to the rear. The narrow by-road was choked full of ewes and lambs, through which he must work his slow way before he could get to the impending slaughter.

Laund seemed to have heard or scented the mongrel before the latter was fairly free from the bushes. For he shot through the huddle of sheep like a flung spear, seeming to swerve not an inch to right nor to left, yet forbearing to jostle one of the dams or their babies.

By the time the mongrel's teeth sought their hold on the panicky lamb, something flashed out of the ruck of the flock and whizzed at him with express-train speed.

Before the mongrel's ravening jaws could close on the woolly throat, young Laund's body had smitten the marauder full in the shoulder, rolling him over in the dust.

For a moment the two battling dogs rolled and revolved and spun on the ground, in a mad tangle that set the yellow dust to flying and scared the sheep into a baaing clump in midroad.

Then the two warriors were on their feet again, rearing, tearing, rending at each other's throats, their snarling voices filling the still afternoon air with horrific din.

The mongrel was almost a third larger than the slender young collie. By sheer weight he bore Laund to earth, snatching avidly at the collie's throat.

But a collie down is not a collie beaten. Catlike, Laund tucked all four feet under him as he fell. Dodging the throat lunge, he leaped up with the resilience of a rubber ball. As he arose, his curved eyetooth scored a razor-gash in the mongrel's underbody and side.

Roaring with rage and pain, the mongrel reared to fling himself on his smaller opponent and to bear him down again by sheer weight. But seldom is a fighting collie caught twice in the same trap.

Downward the mongrel hurled himself. But his adversary was no longer there. Diving under and beyond the larger dog, Laund slashed a second time, cutting to the very bone. Again he and his foe were face to face, foot to foot, tearing and slashing; the collie's speed enabling him to flash in and out and administer thrice as much punishment as he received.

The mongrel gained a grip on the side of Laund's throat. Laund wrenched free, leaving skin and hair in the other's jaws, and dived under again. This time he caught a grip dear to his wolf ancestors. His gleaming teeth seized the side of the mongrel's lower left hindleg.

With a screech the giant dog crashed to the road, hamstrung, helpless. There he lay until Crae's hired man came running up, rifle in hand, and put the brute out of his pain with a bullet through the skull.

For a mere second, Laund stood panting above his fallen enemy. Then seeing the mongrel had no more potentialities for harming the flock, the collie darted among the fast-scattering ewes and lambs, rounding them up and soothing them.

In his brief battle he had fought like a maddened wild beast. Yet now he was once more the lovingly gentle and wise sheepherder, easing and quieting the scared flock as a mother might calm her frightened child.

"Laund!" cried Ronald Crae, delightedly, catching the collie's bleeding head between his calloused hands in a gesture of rough affection. "I was dead wrong. You're as game a dog as ever breathed. It's up to me to apologize for calling you a coward. That cur was as big and husky as a yearling. But you never flinched for a second. You sailed in and licked him. You're *true* game, Laund!"

The panting and bleeding collie wagged his plumed tail ecstatically at the praise and the rare caress. He wiggled and whimpered with joy. Then, of a sudden, he cowered to earth, peering skyward.

Far above flew the forest-ranger's airplane, on the way back from a day's fire-scouting among the hills. With the shrill ki-yi of a kicked puppy, Laund clapped his tail between his legs and bolted for the house. Nor could Crae's fiercest shouts check his flight. He did not halt until he had plunged far under Danny's bed and tucked his nose into the dim corner of the little bedroom.

"Half of that dog ought to have a hero medal!" raged Crae to his wife, as he stamped into the kitchen after he and the hired man had collected the scattered sheep and folded them. "Half of him ought to have a hero medal. And the other half of him ought to be shot, for the rottenest coward I ever set eyes on. His pluck saved me a lamb this afternoon. But his cowardice knocks out any chance of his winning the field trials next month."

"But why? If—"

"The trials are held at the Fairgrounds—the second day of the Fair. There's dead sure to be a dozen airships buzzing around the field all day. There always are. The first one of them Laund sees, he'll drop his work and he'll streak for home, yowling at every jump. I'm due to be laughed out of my boots by the crowd, if I take him there. Yet there isn't another dog in the state that can touch him as a sheep-worker. Rank bad luck, isn't it?"

So it was that Laund's return to favor and to respect was pitifully brief. True, his victory prevented the Craes from continuing to regard him as an out-and-out coward. But the repetition of his flight from the airship all but blotted out the prestige of his fighting prowess.

The sensitive young dog felt the atmosphere of qualified disapproval which surrounded him, and he moped sadly. He knew he had done valiantly in tackling the formidable sheep-killer that had menaced his woolly charges. But he knew, too, that he was in disgrace again for yielding to that unconquerable fear which possessed him at sight of anything soaring in the air above his head.

He lay moping on the shady back porch of the farmhouse one hot morning, some days later. He was unhappy, and the heat made him drowsy. But with one half-shut eye he watched Danny limping painfully to the bantamyard and opening its gate to let his feathered pets out for a run in the grass.

Laund loved Danny as he loved nothing and nobody else. He was the crippled child's worshiping slave, giving to the boy the strangely protective adoration which the best type of collie reserves for the helpless. As a rule he was Danny's devoted shadow at every step the fragile little fellow took. But at breakfast this morning Crae had delivered another tirade on Laund's cowardice, having seen the collie flinch and tremble when a pigeon flew above him in the barnyard. Danny had seen the same thing himself, more than once. But now that his father had seen and condemned it, the child felt a momentary disgust for the cringing dog. Wherefore, when the little fellow had come limping out on the porch between his awkward crutches and Laund had sprung up to follow him, Danny had bidden him crossly to stay where he was. With a sigh the dog had stretched himself out on the porch again, watching the child's slow progress across the yard to the bantam pen.

Danny swung wide the pen door. Out trooped the bantams, willingly following him as he led them to the grassplot. Supporting his weight on one of the two crutches—without which he could neither walk nor stand —he took a handful of crumbs from his pocket and tossed them into the grass for his pets to scramble for.

Laund was not the scene's only watcher. High in the hot blue sky hung two circling specks. From the earth they were almost invisible. But to their keen sight Danny and his scuttling chickens were as visible as they were to Laund himself.

The huge hen hawk and his mate were gaunt from long-continued foraging for their nestlings. Now that the brood was fledged and able to fend for itself, they had time to remember their own unappeased hunger.

For weeks they had eaten barely enough to keep themselves alive. All the rest of their plunder had been carried to a mammoth nest of brown sticks and twigs, high in the top of a mountain-side pine tree; there to be fought over and gobbled by two half-naked, wholly rapacious baby hawks.

Today the two mates were free at last to forage for themselves. But food was scarce. The wild things of woods and meadows had grown wary, through the weeks of predatory hunt for them. Most farmers were keeping their chickens in wire-topped yards. The half-famished pair of hawks had scoured the heaven since dawn in quest of a meal, at every hour growing more ragingly famished.

Now, far below them, they saw the bevy of fat bantams at play in the grass, a full hundred yards from the nearest house. True, a crippled and twisted child stood near them, supported by crutches. But by some odd instinct the half-starved birds seemed to know he was not formidable nor in any way to be feared.

No other human was in sight. Here, unprotected, was a feast of fat fowls. Thrice the hawks circled. Then, by tacit consent, they "stooped." Down through the windless air they clove their way at a speed of something like ninety miles an hour.

One of the bantams lifted its head and gave forth a warning "chir-r-r!" to its fellows. Instantly the brood scattered, with flapping wings and fast-twinkling yellow legs.

Danny stared in amazement. Then something blackish

and huge swept down upon the nearest hen and gripped it. In the same fraction of time the second hawk smote the swaggering little rooster of the flock.

The rooster had turned and bolted to Danny for protection. Almost between the child's helpless feet he crouched. Here it was that the hawk struck him.

Immediately, Danny understood. His beloved flock was raided by hawks. In fury, he swung aloft one of his crutches; and he brought it down with all his puny strength in the direction of the big hawk as it started aloft with the squawking rooster in its talons.

Now, even in a weak grasp, a clubbed and swung crutch is a dangerous weapon. More than one strong man—as police records will show—has been killed by a well-struck blow on the head from such a bludgeon.

Danny smote not only with all his fragile force, but with the added strength of anger. He gripped the crutch by its rubber point and swung it with all his weight as well as with his weak muscular power. The blow was aimed in the general direction of the hawk, as the bird left ground. The hawk's upward spring added to the crutch's momentum. The sharp corner of the armpit crosspiece happened to come in swashing contact with the bird's skull.

The impact of the stroke knocked the crutch out of Danny's hand and upset the child's own equilibrium. To the grass he sprawled, the other crutch falling far out of his reach. There he lay, struggling vainly to rise. One clutching little hand closed on the pinions of the hawk.

The bird had been smitten senseless by the whack of the crutch point against the skull. Though the force had not been great enough to smash the skull or break the neck, yet it had knocked the hawk unconscious for a moment or so. The giant brown bird lay supine, with outstretched wings. Right valorously did the prostrate child seize upon the nearest of these wings.

As he had seen the first hawk strike, Danny had cried aloud in startled defiance at the preying bird. The cry had not reached his mother, working indoors, nor the men who were unloading a wagon of hay into the loft on the far side of the barn. But it had assailed the ears of Laund, even as the collie was shrinking back into the kitchen at far sound of those dreaded rushing wings.

For the barest fraction of an instant Laund crouched,

hesitant. Then again came Danny's involuntary cry and the soft thud of his falling body on the grass. Laund hesitated no longer.

The second hawk was mounting in air, carrying its prey toward the safety of the mountain forests, there to be devoured at leisure. But, looking down, it saw its mate stretched senseless on the ground, the crippled child grasping its wing.

Through the courage of devotion or through contempt for so puny an adversary, the hawk dropped its luscious burden and flew at the struggling Danny.

Again Laund hesitated, though this time only in spirit, for his lithely mighty body was in hurricane motion as he sped to Danny's aid. His heart flinched at sight and sound of those swishing great wings, at the rank scent, and at the ferocious menace of beak and claw. Almost ungovernable was his terror at the stark nearness of these only things in all the world that he feared—these flying scourges he feared to the point of insane panic.

Tremendous was the urge of that mortal terror. But tenfold more urgent upon him was the peril to Danny whom he worshiped.

The child lay, still grasping the wing of the hawk he had so luckily stunned. With his other hand he was preparing to strike the hawk's onrushing mate. The infuriated bird was hurling itself full at Danny's defenseless face, heedless of the ridiculously useless barrier of his outthrust fist. The stunned hawk began to quiver and twist, as consciousness seeped back into its jarred brain.

This was what Laund saw. This was what Laund understood. And the understanding of his little master's hideous danger slew the fear that hitherto had been his most unconquerable impulse.

Straight at the cripple's face flew the hawk. The curved beak and the rending talons were not six inches from Danny's eyes when something big and furry tore past, vaulting the prostrate child and the stunned bird beside him.

With all the speed and skill of his wolf ancestors Laund drove his curved white tusks into the breast of the charging hawk.

Deep clove his eyeteeth, through the armor of feathers, and through the tough breastbone. They ground their way with silent intensity toward a meeting, in the very vitals of the hawk.

The bird bombarded him with its powerful wings, banging him deafeningly and agonizingly about the head and shoulders, hammering his sensitive ears. The curved talons tore at his white chest, ripping deep and viciously. The crooked beak struck for his eyes, again and again, in lightning strokes. Failing to reach them, it slashed the silken top of his head, well-nigh severing one of his furry little tulip ears.

Laund was oblivious to the fivefold punishment, the very hint of which had hitherto been enough to send him ki-yi-ing under Danny's bed. He was not fighting now for himself, but for the child who was at once his ward and his deity.

On himself he was taking the torture that otherwise must have been inflicted on Danny. For perhaps the millionth time in the history of mankind and of dog, the

Scriptural adage was fulfilled, and perfect love was casting out fear.

Then, of a sudden, the punishment ceased. The hawk quivered all over and collapsed inert between Laund's jaws. One of the mightily grinding eyeteeth had pierced its heart.

Laund dropped the carrion carcass; backing away and blinking, as his head buzzed with the bastinade of wing blows it had sustained and with the pain of the beak stab.

But there was no time to get his breath and his bearings. The second hawk had come back to consciousness with a startling and raging suddenness. Finding its wing grasped by a human hand, it was turning fiercely upon the child.

Laund flung himself on the hawk from behind. He attacked just soon enough to deflect the beak from its aim at the boy's eyes and the talons from the boy's puny throat.

His snapping jaws aimed for the hawk's neck, to break it. They missed their mark by less than an inch, tearing out a thick tuft of feathers instead. His white forefeet were planted on the hawk's tail as he struck for the neck.

The bird's charge at Danny was balked, but the hawk itself was not injured. It whirled about on the dog, pecking for the eyes and lambasting his hurt head with its fistlike pinions.

Heedless of the menace, Laund drove in at the furious creature, striking again for the breast. For a few seconds the pair were one scrambling, flapping, snarling, and tumbling mass.

Away from Danny they rolled and staggered in their mad scrimmage. Then Laund ceased to thrash about. He braced himself and stood still. He had found the breast-hold he sought.

For another few moments the climax of the earlier battle was re-enacted. To Danny it seemed as if the bird were beating and ripping his dear pal to death.

Beside himself with wild desire to rescue Laund, and ashamed of his own contempt for the dog's supposed cowardice, Danny writhed to his feet and staggered toward the battling pair, his fists aloft in gallant effort to tear the hawk in two.

Then, as before, came that sudden cessation of wing-beating. The bird quivered spasmodically. Laund let the dead hawk drop from his jaws as he had let drop its mate. Staggering drunkenly up to Danny, he tried to lick the child's tear-spattered face.

From the house and from the barn came the multiple thud of running feet. Mrs. Crae and the men were bearing down upon the scene. They saw a bleeding and reeling dog walking toward them beside a weeping and reeling little boy. From the onlookers went up a wordless and gabbling shout of astonishment.

Danny was walking! without his crutches he was walking; he who had not taken a step by himself since the day he was stricken with the illness that crippled him; he whose parents had been told by the doctors that he could never hope to walk or even to stand up without his crutches!

Yes, he was one of the several hundred children—victims of the same disease and of other nerve-paralysis disorders—who regained the long-lost power over their limbs and muscles, through great shock and supreme effort. But that made the miracle seem none the less a miracle to the Craes and to the former cripple himself.

In the midst of the annual field trials of the National Collie Association, the next month, a gigantic and noisy airplane whirred low over the field where the dogs were at work.

If Laund heard or saw it, he gave it no heed. He went unerringly and calmly and snappily ahead with his tests —until he won the Grand Prize.

He saw no reason to feel scared or even interested when the airship cast its winked shadow across him. A few weeks earlier he had fought and conquered two of those same flappy things. He had proved to himself, forever, that there was nothing about them to be afraid of.

Gun-Shy

by Edward Fenton

EVERY DAY the mornings in the country turned chillier. The sycamore outside the kitchen window was soon bright yellow, and the trees all down the lane made a high arch of burning colors. When Joel stepped out of the house his breathing made little cold clouds of white vapor in front of his face.

This morning he was early. Muggsy hadn't even finished his cereal yet. The Duchess ran ahead of him sniffing the air excitedly. With a sudden bound she dashed off into the meadow. Joel watched her weaving through the tall, dry grass, her nose to the ground one moment and the next minute springing up like a jack rabbit, her black ears flying.

Then, suddenly, there was a rustling noise and a mass of feathers rose from the clump of grass ahead over their heads. It glistened across the autumn landscape. Then it was winging out of sight!

The Duchess, now standing stiff in the middle of the

field like a dog painted on a calendar picture, was looking after it too. When the bird could no longer be seen, she galumphed back to Joel's side.

Henry came toward them from the barn. Joel noticed at once that he had on his old leather hunting jacket, with the celluloid window on the back of it for his hunting license. Pushed back on his head was a red cap with a visor.

"Hi, Henry," Joel said. "Are you going out today?"

"It's the first day of huntin'," Henry asserted. "Ain't missed it in years. Don't reckon I'll miss it today. Got my license, got my gun all oiled back there in th' barn. Ought to be a good day."

"There are lots of birds around this year," Joel said. "The Duchess just flushed one a minute ago. It was a beauty! It went over that way." He pointed toward the Rocky Pasture.

Henry nodded. "I seen it," he said. "As a matter of fact," he went on, "I was thinkin' of takin' the Duchess along. Ain't never tried her out in the field as yet. Might's well see if she's any good or not."

"I'll bet she'll be better than any other dog you ever took hunting," Joel said stoutly. "Won't you, Duch?"

The Duchess, however, was much too busy pursuing a flea near the base of her tail to do anything in reply to Joel's question.

The porch door slammed just then.

"Well, here's ol' Muggsy, the great trapper!" Henry called out, swinging him up on his shoulder. Anthony had on a scarlet hunter's cap like Henry's. He looked very proud of it.

"You bet!" Muggsy began. "I'm the best hunter for miles," he announced with no attempt at modesty. "I can catch lions, 'n' bears, 'n'—well, anything, 'cause I'm—"

"Oh, come on," Joel said impatiently. "I've got to get you to school. The bus'll be here soon."

They started down the lane together. Joel called back over his shoulder, "Have a good day, Henry. You and the Duchess!"

"Sure," Henry called back. "We'll make out fine together. So long!"

Johnny Nesbitt was in the bus when Joel and Muggsy clambered in. They all sat together, looking out the window. From time to time they could see men, sometimes singly, sometimes in groups, walking along the road. All of them carried guns and had their hunting licenses pinned to their jackets where everyone could see them, and they all wore bright red caps so that other hunters would not mistake them for game as they moved through the woods. Most of them had dogs following along after them.

"Rusty's a good hunter," Johnny Nesbitt said. "He can smell a rabbit a mile way."

"Henry's taking the Duchess out with him," Joel told him in reply. "She's a real hunting dog. I'll bet when I get home Henry'll have so many pheasants he won't hardly be able to carry them all!"

That day school seemed to drag on without end. All through the classes Joel's attention wandered off from his books or the blackboard to the windows. The trees outside blazed against the clear November sky. From time to time he could hear in the distance the sharp crack-

crack of a rifle or the high, excited barking of a dog. All his thoughts were with Henry and the Duchess.

The Duchess, so far, had not done anything to demonstrate her true caliber. She hadn't rescued anyone yet, or had a chance to prove herself a heroine. But this time, he knew, she would show her true colors!

The school bus going home seemed to take all afternoon. Why did the driver always have to stop forever, and why did it always take the other kids such a long time to get off? At last it came to a halt with a squeaking of brakes beside the blue letter box marked "Evans."

Joel looked for the Duchess. Usually she knew when it was time for the bus to return, and she sat in the middle of the lane waiting for him. But she wasn't there now. "She's probably still out with Henry," Joel thought, although it did seem odd that Henry would be out hunting all day, and it was now nearly milking time.

He ran up the lane to the house. Muggsy had to puff like a locomotive to keep up with him.

No, the Duchess wasn't anywhere around. And there was Henry, going out to the barn.

"Henry, Henry!" Joel cried. "Where is she?"

Henry set down the pails he was carrying.

"Dunno, Joey," he replied slowly.

"Well, didn't you go out hunting and all?"

Henry nodded. "Sure we went out," he said. "She was fine too. Got a good nose on her. In fact she was all right until I raised my gun and fired."

Joel was breathless. "And then what happened?"

"First thing I know there wasn't no Duchess there. She ran off faster'n I could see her go. Looked all over for her. Looked for hours, but I never did find her. Had to come back 'count of it being milking time." Henry put his big hand on Joel's shoulder. "I'm sorry, kid," he said. "I wouldn't have taken her if I'd of known. She's what they call *gun-shy*. She's scared of shootin'."

"But—but where's she now? We've got to find her!" Joel blinked hard.

"No way of tellin'," Henry said, shaking his head. "She's probably hidin' somewhere right now. She won't come back for a while. The woods are full of gunfire."

Supper was dismal. Joel could hardly swallow, and after every few choking mouthfuls he ran out to the porch to whistle. "She might be out there now," he explained.

Mama looked up at the ceiling. "Boys and dogs!" she sighed. "They're the bane of my life!"

But when Joel came back she looked up hopefully. When he shook his head she sighed again, only it was a different kind of sigh.

Muggsy suddenly announced: "Hey, Joey, I got a idea!"

"Can't you *ever* leave me alone, ever?" Joel demanded. "I'm thinking."

"Well, I been thinking too," Muggsy persisted. "I been thinking about how I found her. I betcha you ain't looked under the bridge!"

Joel looked up in amazement. "I never thought of that!" he exclaimed. The next moment he had dashed out of the dining room.

"Put on your jacket!" Mama called, but the front door had already slammed behind him. "Oh, no, you don't,

Anthony!" she said firmly as Muggsy began to squirm off his chair. "You're staying right here."

Joel ran headlong into Henry, who had been out in the barn. "I'm goin'—down to the bridge," he panted. "To see if she's there."

Henry went along with him. They whistled for her at every other step, but there was no Duchess to come dashing up to them in response. They went down the lane together. Joel clenched his fists until his fingernails dug into his palms.

But under the bridge there was nothing: just the creek trickling in the dark and the stones shining with wetness when the flashlight went on. Joel had never felt so miserable. "Perhaps she got shot, Henry."

"Dunno," Henry said. He shrugged his shoulders and switched off his flashlight. "Come on, kid, better get back. It's cold out here without your sweater. Your ma won't like it. And it won't bring Her Highness back, just standing here and shivering."

They climbed up to the road again and began trudging back to the house.

Suddenly Joel stopped. "Listen!" he whispered.

They stopped. There was a faint pattering sound. It grew louder as they waited.

"Sure it's her!" Joel cried.

And it was indeed the Duchess. She came toward them at a tired trot. Joel ran forward and put his arms around her. He could feel the burrs sticking to her coat. She was trembling.

Joel looked up at Henry. "Henry, remember when we

first found her? Do you think she might have run off that time the same way? I mean—"

Henry shook his head. "Dunno," he said. "Cain't never tell. Could be."

"But—but that means she's no good for hunting, doesn't it?" Joel thought of Johnny Nesbitt's Rusty, and of how he himself had boasted of the Duchess. He swallowed hard. "But I don't care, Henry," he said, running his hands through the shivering dog's coat. "She needs us more than ever now, and there are worse things than being afraid of guns, aren't there, Henry? Aren't there?"

"Sure," Henry said thoughtfully. "Sure. Lots worse things."

Joel stroked the Duchess. "See, Duch," he told her, "it's all right now. You're home again." He felt as though something inside him was choking him. But he was happy that he had found her again.

"Come on, Henry," he said. "Let's run back. It's cold out tonight."

On Saturday afternoon Joel Evans and Johnny Nesbitt lay spread out, faces downward, upon a nest of dry leaves. Noisily they munched at a couple of frostbitten apples from the basketful which they had gathered for Johnny's mother. Juice dribbled icily down Joel's chin. "I like 'em best this way," he announced indistinctly.

In the deep grass, not far away, waited their four-legged shadows: Johnny's Airedale Rusty and the Duchess. Both were panting gently. From time to time one of them stirred, making a dry rattling sound among the crisp leaves.

It was almost evening. The air was getting keen. The faces of the boys were raw from the wind. Their eyes shone. Their ears and the tips of their noses tingled.

It had been an exhausting Saturday, and all four of them were tired. Not that they had, any of them, much to show for it. Sure enough, there was the basket of apples for Mrs. Nesbitt. It had been fun climbing the trees and shaking them down, while the dogs barked furiously at the rain of fruit which thudded and plummeted to the hard ground. And there was a pleasant aching in their arms and legs from all the fields they had scrambled across, the brooks they had jumped over (one of Joel's socks was wet from the time he had missed), the gullies and ravines they had explored all through the sharp, sun-shot day.

For the dogs there were the thousands of exciting smells to remember and the miles of countless mysterious tracks which they had pursued, yipping frantically. Knowingly, they rolled their brown eyes at their masters.

Joel turned his head and stared at the darkening sky. "Gosh, Johnny, it's getting late. I'd better think of making tracks before Mama sends out a posse." He stretched lazily, then rolled back on the ground, folding his arms behind his head.

"My mother'll be worrying too," Johnny said. "It's funny; she knows I'm all right. Nothing ever happens to me. But she always worries just the same. She ought to be used to me by now!"

"I know," Joel agreed. "They ought to relax more, but they never do. I guess that's the way they are. You just can't change them."

They both lay there, wondering why mothers worried the way they did. But neither of them stirred an inch to get up and start home.

The Duchess pulled herself out of her bed of leaves, stretched luxuriously, yawned with a great creaking of her jaws, and looked at Rusty to see what he was doing. He was engrossed in the serious business of licking a forepaw. The Duchess turned her back to him and moseyed over to where Joel lay.

Joel scratched her chin. "How's the girl?" he demanded. "How's Her Highness?" In reply, she licked his face until he had to raise himself, laughing, to a sitting position.

Johnny got up then, too. They both sat among the

dead leaves of the past summer and wondered where the day had gone to.

"It's been one super day," Joel said. He looked around him, at the dark trees against the setting sun. Below them —it seemed far, far below, although he knew it was only a few minutes' run—snuggled the Nesbitt farmhouse. The lights were already on. The windows glowed yellow and smoke twisted from the chimney. He picked another apple out of the basket and bit into it.

It was a good apple, firm and juicy. Joel looked at Johnny and winked; Johnny winked back. Then Joel looked at the Duchess. She had her head slightly to one side and her brown eyes were regarding him with all the trust and faith in the world. Suddenly Joel felt an overwhelming contentment sweep over him. It didn't matter about her being gun-shy, about anything. It was just perfect sitting there with her and Johnny as the sun was setting, and eating an apple. It was a moment he wanted to make last forever. "Stop, clock," he wanted to shout. "Just leave your hands where they are for a while."

Finally he said, and it seemed to him as though his voice came out strangely quiet and small, "I don't know any other place I'd rather be than right here now. Do you, Johnny?"

"Sure," Johnny said. "Lots of places. Top of the Empire State Building in New York. Or flying over Shangri-La in my own B-29. The *Johnny N* I'd call it, and I'd have the name painted right on her, big. That's the life!" Johnny's eyes began to glisten with excitement.

"Or I'd like to be in a foxhole at the front with a little

old machine gun cradled in my arms. Rattatatattat! I'd show that enemy a thing or two or three. They could shoot and shoot at me all they liked. They'd only miss. I wouldn't even hear it! Then me and Rusty—he'd be my Specially Trained Combat Dog—we'd jump out of that foxhole and give them the rush. Just the two of us; we'd take them all prisoners." Johnny clicked his tongue. "That's where I'd like to be. Not stuck out here where it's the same thing all the time, no excitement.

"And what's more," he added, in a confidential tone, "as soon as I'm old enough to do it, I'm gonna join up. And Rusty's coming right with me. I'll bet they could use a smart dog like him in the Army. He's so tough I bet he could easy get into the Marines!"

Joel was scratching the Duchess slowly behind the ear. He didn't say anything.

"Hey, Joey," Johnny went on—he grew more and more excited as the idea became clearer—"you could come too. How'd you like that? And take the Duchess!" He looked eagerly at Joel. "What do you think of that?"

The look on Joel's face stopped Johnny short. "Oh, gee, Joey, I forgot about the Duchess. I mean, about her bein'—"

Joel jumped to his feet. "Oh, that's all right, Johnny. We sort of had other plans anyway." He tried to sound offhand. "And, anyway, we have to start trekking home now. I guess it's pretty late."

"Sure," Johnny said. "Sure. And my mother will give it to me good if I don't get those apples home to her!"

Johnny and Rusty walked Joel and the Duchess as far as the glen in silence.

"So long, Johnny," Joel called as he turned off. "See you Monday."

"So long," Johnny called back.

The faint trail across the glen was the shortest way home and Joel wanted to get there before dark. The sun was pretty low already.

The Duchess was off after some scent in a clump of bushes. Her nose was to the ground and her white plume of a tail cut through the twilight. Joel whistled to her. She paid no attention to his call.

Joel's mellow mood of happiness and contentment had completely vanished. In its place he was seized by an unreasoning rage.

He whistled again. She was utterly useless, he thought furiously. A gun-shy bird dog. Everybody laughed at her. And now she wouldn't even obey him when he whistled!

"Come here, you!" he shouted harshly.

She bolted out of the bushes and came toward him. Through the growing twilight he could see how uncertain and surprised she was. Already he felt a faint twinge of shame for having spoken to her as he had. But the senseless anger still boiled inside him.

"You come straight off, the next time I call you," he said gruffly.

Then he struck off across the glen toward home. He stopped at one place long enough to cut a maple switch. As he went on, he slashed viciously now and again at the dark trunks of the trees he passed. The Duchess followed faithfully at his heel. He could hear her pattering evenly behind him but he did not turn his head once or stop to speak to her.

By the time Joel reached home, darkness had already fallen. All the lights of the house were on. From the outside, everything had a warm and friendly look.

"We'll catch it for being late," Joel muttered to the Duchess. Resignedly, he made his way to the back door.

Alma was flying about in the kitchen like a demented banshee. She paused long enough to glance up when Joel came in. "Oh, there you are!" she exclaimed. To Joel's surprise, her voice wasn't at all scolding. "Hurry on upstairs and put on your good pants and a clean shirt," she said. "Dinner'll be on soon. You don't want to be late for it."

"I thought I was late already," he said. Then he noticed that she was wearing her best apron, the one with the white ruffles starched as stiff as cardboard.

"Zowie!" he cried. "What's up? Lord Mayor invite himself for dinner?"

"Never you mind," Alma replied. She pushed him to the door and waved him up the staircase. "I've got work to do. You'll find out what's up soon enough when you come down again."

Joel scratched his head and started up the stairs. Halfway up he had a sudden idea. "It's not Ellen home for the weekend, is it, Alma?" he called hopefully down the stair well.

"It is not," Alma called back. "And don't forget to comb your hair and take that scrubbing brush to your nails," she added. "I'll go tell your ma you'll be right down."

While Joel changed his clothes and washed, the Duchess pattered after him from his bedroom to the bathroom and back again. He could hear, faintly, voices floating up from the living room. He wondered what was happening. At first he decided that Mr. and Mrs. Grant had come to dinner. But then Alma wouldn't have put on her best apron just for them. Maybe it was an important business friend of Papa's.

"Dr. Watson, I am compelled to admit that I am completely baffled this time," Joel said, frowning into the mirror. Then, after a brief tussle between his cowlick and his brush (the cowlick won), he switched off the light and went downstairs to the living room.

He saw Mama first. She had on a long dress and her heavy silver Indian bracelets. She was saying something which he couldn't hear and she smiled as she spoke. She looked different from the way she did every day. Joel had forgotten how young and pretty his mother could look. Papa stood behind her, beaming.

Mama turned her head and saw Joel. "And here's Joey!" she announced. Laughing gaily, she pulled him into the room.

Then, suddenly, Joel realized why Alma was wearing her number-one starched apron and why Mama had on her long dress and such a radiant look and why even Papa was smiling openly. Leaning against the mantelpiece, his back to the fire, stood a tall, grinning young man in the khaki uniform of a lieutenant.

"Uncle Seymour!"

The grin widened. "Hi, Joey!"

It was a long time since Joel had seen his uncle. That had been before Uncle Seymour had gone overseas. Joel ran forward. He wanted to rush up and throw his arms around his uncle. But when he came up to him, Joel suddenly stiffened self-consciously and held out his hand instead.

Gravely they shook hands.

Muggsy, who had been quiet and awed, suddenly came to life. "Look, Joey," he cried. "He's got a gold bar on his shoulder. That means he's an officer now. And lookit all the medals he won." Muggsy stood on his tiptoes, running his forefinger across the row of service ribbons pinned to his uncle's tunic. "This one's for Good Conduck. This one's for—"

"Anthony!" Mama said. "Must you always handle everything you see?"

"I was only showing Joey!"

"Well, Joel can see for himself."

Joel could indeed see for himself. His uncle seemed to be taller, somehow, than last time. His face had a lean, almost tired look about it. Joel's eyes took in every detail of the uniform, with its knife-sharp creases, the gold insignia and the row of ribbons. On one of the ribbons there were little stars. They stood for battles, Joel knew.

His uncle was smiling. "Don't pay any mind to those ribbons, Joey," he said. "They're only my brag rags. Fruit salad, we call 'em."

Joel smiled back at him. "Gosh, Uncle Seymour—I mean Lieutenant!—it's good to see you. When did you get back?"

"I hopped a plane over there only three days ago, and here I am!"

Papa began to whistle "Off we go into the wild blue yonder." He caught Uncle Seymour's eye and they both began to laugh.

"Oh, Charlie!" Mama wailed. "There you go. I don't see where that's so funny. Honestly, when you two get together, you carry on just like a couple of overgrown schoolboys."

That only made them laugh harder. "Listen to Grandma!" Uncle Seymour roared. "Relax, Ellie. You look too pretty tonight to pull that stern, serious stuff on us!"

Then Mama gave him a little push. "You!" she said, and she began to laugh too. She didn't look much older than Ellen right then! Joel and Muggsy looked on, grinning. The whole room seemed to be full of happiness and warmth and laughter.

There were candles on the dinner table. Whenever Alma came in, Uncle Seymour teased her and made her blush, but Joel decided that she really liked it, especially when he got up and made a speech.

He said in his speech that he wanted to be on record as being duly, properly, and thoroughly appreciative. Alma had outdone herself as an exponent of the culinary art and Uncle Seymour knew personally of several regiments that would have given their collective eyeteeth to have had her with them overseas.

"Aw, go on with all your talk!" said Alma. She got as red in the face as a poppy, but she loved every word of it.

They remained at table a long time. Papa asked Uncle Seymour a great many serious questions, and Joel didn't dare interrupt. Muggsy tried to several times, but Papa's most sarcastic tone of voice managed to squelch him.

Finally Mama rose, which was the signal for them to

go back to the living room. The Duchess was already there, comfortably ensconced on the rug in front of the snapping fire.

"Well, look who's here!" Uncle Seymour said. He turned to Mr. Evans. "Charlie, I thought you hated dogs. Where'd you ever pick this one up?"

"I still abominate the noisome yapping creatures," Mr. Evans answered. "This particularly ill-favored specimen happens to be a waif. It is only suffered on the premises because for some mysterious reason my children seem to have become hysterically attached to it."

"She's a beauty," Uncle Seymour said. He knelt and stroked her warm hair. She thumped her tail lazily against the floor.

"I found her," Muggsy said. "She was under the bridge and I found her!" Between them, the Evanses poured out the story of how the Duchess came to be with them.

"So!" Uncle Seymour said. He turned to Mr. Evans. "And is she a good hunter, Charlie?" he asked.

Joel swallowed hard. What would Uncle Seymour think if he found out the truth about her? It didn't matter with most people. But Uncle Seymour was different. Besides, he was a soldier.

Tensely, Joel watched his father and waited to hear what he would say.

Mr. Evans cleared his throat.

"Charlie!" Mama said warningly.

Joel didn't dare to swallow again.

"Hm," Papa said. "Well, as a matter of fact—hm—to tell the precise truth—I haven't had her out in the field myself, so—hm—I couldn't exactly testify."

Joel shot his father a grateful glance.

But they had reckoned without Muggsy. The youngest Evans had never been at a loss for words. This time was no exception.

"But Henry took her out, Uncle Seymour. And do you know what? She ran away. She's gun-shy!" He turned triumphantly to his brother. "Isn't she, Joel?"

It was Mama who broke the ensuing silence.

"Up to bed with you," she said. "This very minute," she added. It was her firmest tone of voice. From past experience, Muggsy knew that it was the one Mama used when she Meant Every Word She Said.

With a carefully assumed "I-don't-care" look on his face, Muggsy got up from the footstool where he had been sitting and started for the stairs. Uncle Seymour's voice, booming across the room, stopped him in his tracks.

"What I want to know is, what's so awful about being gun-shy?"

Muggsy turned and looked around at his uncle. His eyes were wary with suspicion.

"I'm gun-shy myself," said Uncle Seymour. Joel gaped incredulously at the bright ribbons awarded for valor which were pinned to his uncle's chest.

"Yes, Joey," his uncle said. "You can look at those all you like. But in spite of them I'm still gun-shy. Most of us were, although we didn't always admit it. It scared the dickens out of us when those big guns used to go off. Only there we were, and there was nothing we could do about it, so we had to be heroes."

"But—but—" Joel stammered.

"Sure, after a while we got used to it," his uncle said

more quietly. "But if I'd have been able to bolt the first time, I'd have gone like a lubricated lightning streak. And practically all the other men with me would have, too."

Joel and Anthony stared at him.

Their uncle's voice lowered to a confidential whisper. "And you know, even though it's all over, I still dream about those guns sometimes." He thoughtfully shook his head. "And take it from me, chum, those are pretty bad dreams to have."

Mama broke in. "Seymour," she said, "I do think it's time they went to bed. Both of them, in fact. It's been a big night, and there's all tomorrow ahead of us."

After Joel and Muggsy had said good night and started up the stairs, the Duchess got up and cocked her head after them. Then, wagging her tail, she made her way up to bed behind Joel.

Long after Muggsy had fallen asleep Joel lay awake in the dark, staring at the ceiling. He was trying to make up his mind about what Uncle Seymour had said.

It was hard to figure out exactly. There was something funny somewhere.

Imagine admitting that you were afraid of guns and battle and all that kind of thing! Especially when you were a soldier! He would never have dreamed of admitting to Johnny Nesbitt that he had often wondered just how exciting being a real soldier would be. But Joel had always had his private doubts.

And now it was Uncle Seymour who had confirmed them! And he was no coward. He'd been through plenty, and he knew what it was like if anyone did, Joel guessed. Joel lay staring at the dark ceiling, trying to imagine what

Uncle Seymour had gone through those nights when he lay in his foxhole with the guns going off all around him. The quiet room became alive with imaginary tracer bullets spitting from planes and the whine of artillery shells.

Joel's arms stole around the Duchess. She was breathing quietly in her sleep. Somehow everything had changed around. It was as though a weight which had been pressing against his chest had been miraculously lifted. He wasn't going to be ashamed of her any more for something she couldn't help.

"Well, Duch," he whispered, "I guess there are lots worse things than being gun-shy." He was sure of that now.

Old Yeller

by Fred Gipson

THAT LITTLE ARLISS! If he wasn't a mess! From the time he'd grown up big enough to get out of the cabin, he made a practice of trying to catch and keep every living thing that ran, flew, jumped or crawled.

Every night before Mama let him go to bed, she'd make Arliss empty his pockets of whatever he'd captured during the day. Generally, it would be a tangled-up mess of grasshoppers and worms and praying bugs and little rusty tree lizards. One time he brought in a horned toad that got so mad he swelled out round and flat as a Mexican *tortilla* and bled at the eyes. Sometimes it was stuff like a young bird that had fallen out of its nest before it could fly, or a green-speckled spring frog or a striped water snake. And once he turned out of his pocket a wadded-up baby copperhead that nearly threw Mama into spasms. We never did figure out why the snake hadn't bitten him, but Mama took no more chances on snakes. Then she made me spend better than a week, taking him out and teaching him to throw rocks and kill snakes.

That was all right with Little Arliss. If Mama wanted him to kill his snakes first, he'd kill them. But that still didn't keep him from sticking them in his pockets along with everything else he'd captured that day. The snakes might be stinking by the time Mama called on him to empty his pockets, but they'd be dead.

Then, after the yeller dog came, Little Arliss started catching even bigger game. Like cottontail rabbits and chaparral birds and a baby possum that sulked and lay like dead for the first several hours until he finally decided that Arliss wasn't going to hurt him.

Of course, it was Old Yeller that was doing the catching. He'd run the game down and turn it over to Little Arliss. Then Little Arliss could come in and tell Mama a big fib about how he caught it himself.

I watched them one day when they caught a blue catfish out of Birdsong Creek. The fish had fed out into water so shallow that his top fin was sticking out. About the time I saw it, Old Yeller and Little Arliss did, too. They made a run at it. The fish went scooting away toward deeper water, only Yeller was too fast for him. He pounced on the fish and shut his big mouth down over it and went romping to the bank, where he dropped it down on the grass and let it flop. And here came Little Arliss to fall on it like I guess he'd been doing everything else. The minute he got his hands on it, the fish finned him and he went to crying.

But he wouldn't turn the fish loose. He just grabbed **it** up and went running and squawling toward the house,

where he gave the fish to Mama. His hands were all
bloody by then, where the fish had finned him. They
swelled up and got mighty sore; not even a mesquite
thorn hurts as bad as a sharp fish fin when it's run deep
into your hand.

But as soon as Mama had wrapped his hands in a poul-
tice of mashed-up prickly-pear root to draw out the
poison, Little Arliss forgot all about his hurt. And that
night when we ate the fish for supper, he told the biggest
windy I ever heard about how he'd dived 'way down into
a deep hole under the rocks and dragged that fish out and
nearly got drowned before he could swim to the bank
with it.

But when I tried to tell Mama what really happened,
she wouldn't let me. "Now, this is Arliss's story," she said.
"You let him tell it the way he wants to."

I told Mama then, I said: "Mama, that old yeller dog
is going to make the biggest liar in Texas out of Little
Arliss."

But Mama just laughed at me, like she always laughed
at Little Arliss's big windies after she'd gotten off where
he couldn't hear her. She said for me to let Little Arliss
alone. She said that if he ever told a bigger whopper than
the ones I used to tell, she had yet to hear it.

Well, I hushed then. If Mama wanted Little Arliss to
grow up to be the biggest liar in Texas, I guessed it wasn't
any of my business.

All of which, I figure, is what led up to Little Arliss's
catching the bear. I think Mama had let him tell so many
big yarns about catching live game that he'd begun to
believe them himself.

When it happened, I was down the creek a ways, splitting rails to fix up the yard fence where the bulls had torn it down. I'd been down there since dinner, working in a stand of tall slim post oaks. I'd chop down a tree, trim off the branches as far up as I wanted, then cut away the rest of the top. After that I'd start splitting the log.

I'd split the log by driving wedges into the wood. I'd start at the end and hammer in a wedge with the back side of my ax. This would start a little split running lengthways of the log. Then I'd take a second wedge and drive it into this split. This would split the log farther along and, at the same time, loosen the first wedge. I'd then knock the first wedge loose and move it up in front of the second one.

Driving one wedge ahead of the other like that, I could finally split a log in two halves. Then I'd go to work on the halves, splitting them apart. That way, from each log, I'd come out with four rails.

Swinging that chopping ax was sure hard work. The sweat poured off me. My back muscles ached. The ax got so heavy I could hardly swing it. My breath got harder and harder to breathe.

An hour before sundown, I was worn down to a nub. It seemed like I couldn't hit another lick. Papa could have lasted till past sundown, but I didn't see how I could. I shouldered my ax and started toward the cabin, trying to think up some excuse to tell Mama to keep her from knowing I was played clear out.

That's when I heard Little Arliss scream.

Well, Little Arliss was a screamer by nature. He'd scream when he was happy and scream when he was mad and a lot of times he'd scream just to hear himself make a noise. Generally, we paid no more mind to his screaming that we did to the gobble of a wild turkey.

But this time was different. The second I heard his screaming, I felt my heart flop clear over. This time I knew Little Arliss was in real trouble.

I tore up the trail leading toward the cabin. A minute before, I'd been so tired out with my rail splitting that I couldn't have struck a trot. But now I raced through the tall trees in that creek bottom, covering ground like a scared wolf.

Little Arliss's second scream, when it came, was louder and shriller and more frantic-sounding than the first. Mixed with it was a whimpering crying sound that I knew didn't come from him. It was a sound I'd heard before and seemed like I ought to know what it was, but right then I couldn't place it.

Then, from way off to one side came a sound that I would have recognized anywhere. It was the coughing roar of a charging bear. I'd just heard it once in my life. That was the time Mama had shot and wounded a hog-killing bear and Papa had had to finish it off with a knife to keep it from getting her.

My heart went to pushing up into my throat, nearly choking off my wind. I strained for every lick of speed I could get out of my running legs. I didn't know what sort of fix Little Arliss had got himself into, but I knew that it had to do with a mad bear, which was enough.

The way the late sun slanted through the trees had the trail all cross-banded with streaks of bright light and dark shade. I ran through these bright and dark patches so fast that the changing light nearly blinded me. Then suddenly, I raced out into the open where I could see ahead. And what I saw sent a chill clear through to the marrow of my bones.

There was Little Arliss, down in that spring hole again. He was lying half in and half out of the water, holding onto the hind leg of a little black bear cub no bigger than a small coon. The bear cub was out on the bank, whimpering and crying and clawing the rocks with all three of his other feet, trying to pull away. But Little Arliss was holding on for all he was worth, scared now and screaming his head off. Too scared to let go.

How come the bear cub ever came to prowl close enough for Little Arliss to grab him, I don't know. And why he didn't turn on him and bite loose, I couldn't figure out, either. Unless, like Little Arliss, he was too scared to think.

But all of that didn't matter now. What mattered was the bear cub's mama. She'd heard the cries of her baby and was coming to save him. She was coming so fast that she had the brush popping and breaking as she crashed through and over it. I could see her black heavy figure piling off down the slant on the far side of Birdsong Creek. She was roaring mad and ready to kill.

And worst of all, I could see that I'd never get there in time!

Mama couldn't either. She'd heard Arliss, too, and here she came from the cabin, running down the slant toward the spring, screaming at Arliss, telling him to turn the bear cub loose. But Little Arliss wouldn't do it. All he'd do was hang with that hind leg and let out one shrill

shriek after another as fast as he could suck in a breath.

Now the she bear was charging across the shallows in the creek. She was knocking sheets of water high in the bright sun, charging with her fur up and her long teeth bared, filling the canyon with that awful coughing roar. And no matter how fast Mama ran or how fast I ran, the she bear was going to get there first!

I think I nearly went blind then, picturing what was going to happen to Little Arliss. I know that I opened my mouth to scream and not any sound came out.

Then, just as the bear went lunging up the creek bank toward Little Arliss and her cub, a flash of yellow came streaking out of the brush.

It was that big yeller dog. He was roaring like a mad bull. He wasn't one-third as big and heavy as the she bear, but when he piled into her from one side, he rolled her clear off her feet. They went down in a wild, roaring tangle of twisting bodies and scrambling feet and slashing fangs.

As I raced past them, I saw the bear lunge up to stand on her hind feet like a man while she clawed at the body of the yeller dog hanging to her throat. I didn't wait to see more. Without ever checking my stride, I ran in and jerked Little Arliss loose from the cub. I grabbed him by the wrist and yanked him up out of that water and slung him toward Mama like he was a half-empty sack of corn. I screamed at Mama, "Grab him, Mama! Grab him and run!" Then I swung my chopping ax high and wheeled, aiming to cave in the she bear's head with the first lick.

But I never did strike. I didn't need to. Old Yeller hadn't let the bear get close enough. He couldn't handle her; she was too big and strong for that. She'd stand there on her hind feet, hunched over, and take a roaring swing at him with one of those big front claws. She'd slap him head over heels. She'd knock him so far that it didn't look like he could possibly get back there before she charged again, but he always did. He'd hit the ground rolling, yelling his head off with the pain of the blow;

but somehow he'd always roll to his feet. And here he'd come again, ready to tie into her for another round.

I stood there with my ax raised, watching them for a long moment. Then from up toward the house I heard Mama calling: "Come away from there, Travis. Hurry, son! Run!"

That spooked me. Up till then I'd been ready to tie into that bear myself. Now, suddenly, I was scared out of my wits again. I ran toward the cabin.

But like it was, Old Yeller nearly beat me there. I didn't see it, of course; but Mama said that the minute Old Yeller saw we were in the clear and out of danger, he threw the fight to that she bear and lit out for the house. The bear chased him for a little piece, but at the rate Old Yeller was leaving her behind, Mama said it looked like the bear was backing up.

But if the big yeller dog was scared or hurt in any way when he came dashing into the house, he didn't show it. He sure didn't show it like we all did. Little Arliss had hushed his screaming, but he was trembling all over and clinging to Mama like he'd never let her go. And Mama was sitting in the middle of the floor, holding him up close and crying like she'd never stop. And me, I was close to crying, myself.

Old Yeller, though, all he did was come bounding in to jump on us and lick us in the face and bark so loud that there, inside the cabin, the noise nearly made us deaf.

The way he acted, you might have thought that bear fight hadn't been anything more than a rowdy romp that we'd all taken part in for the fun of it.

Mine Enemy's Dog

by Ben Ames Williams

WESTLEY HAD A DOG, a setter, clean-blooded, from one of the country's finest kennels. A New York man who had shot woodcock with the warden the year before had sent the dog as a friendly gift, and Westley accepted it in the same spirit. In its second year and still untrained, it had nevertheless won Westley and won his wife and his children. They all loved the dog, as they loved each other. . . .

Originally this dog had been called Rex. The Westleys changed this name to Reck, which may be short for Reckless, or may be a name by itself. At any rate, it pleased them, and it pleased the dog. . . .

The dog was untrained, and Westley had no time for the arduous work of training. He had meant to send Reck, this fall, to Hepperton, in Liberty; but, to make his amends to Proutt, he took the latter aside this night and asked Proutt to take the training of the dog.

On longer consideration, he might not have done this;

but Westley was a man of impulse, and he was anxious to keep Proutt as a friend. Nevertheless, he had no sooner asked Proutt to take the dog than he regretted it, and hoped Proutt would refuse. But the dog trainer only gave a moment to slow consideration, with downcast eyes.

Then he said huskily: "I charge fifty dollars."

"Sure," said Westley.

"He's a well-blooded dog," said Proutt. "I'll come to-morrow and fetch him."

And with no further word—they were outside the store —he drove away. Westley, watching him go, was filled with vague disquiet. He wished he might withdraw; he wished Proutt would change his mind; he wished the trainer might not come next day. . . .

But Proutt did come, and Westley himself bade Reck into the trainer's buggy and watched the dog ride away with wistful eyes turned backward.

Westley's wife was more concerned than he; and he forgot his own anxiety in reassuring her.

There are a thousand methods for the training of a bird dog, and each man prefers his own. There are some dogs that need much training; there are others that require little or none.

Reck was so nobly blooded that the instincts of his craft were deeply embedded in him. On his first day in the alder swamps with Proutt he proved himself to the full. Proutt was a dog beater, as all men knew, but he did not beat dogs which obeyed him, and he did not beat Reck. This first day he was merely trying the dog.

Reck found a bird, and took stanch point, steady as a rock. It was not yet October, the season was not yet open;

and so Proutt had no right to shoot. Nevertheless he did walk up this bird, and flushed it from where it lay six feet before Reck's nose, and knocked it over before it topped the alders.

Reck stood at point till the bird rose; when its whistling wings lifted it, his nose followed it upward, followed its fall. But he did not stir, did not break shot; and Proutt, watching, knew that this was indeed a dog.

When the bird had fallen, Proutt said softly: "Reck! Fetch dead bird."

Now, this is in some measure the test of a setter. There are many setters that take a natural point and hold it; there are some few that are also natural retrievers, without training. Reck had been taught by Westley's children to fetch sticks or rocks at command. He knew the word.

He went swiftly forward and brought the woodcock, scarce ruffled, and laid it in Proutt's hand. And Proutt took the bird, and stood still, looking down at Reck with a darkly brooding face. Considering, weighing. . . . After a little he began to curse softly, under his breath; and he turned and stamped out of the alder run, and bade Reck to heel, and went home. And Reck trotted at his heels, tongue out, panting happily. . . .

There are many ways by which the Devil may come at a man. One of them is through hatred, and another way is to put a helpless thing in that man's hands. If the good in him outweighs the bad, well enough; but if the evil has ascendancy, then that man is utterly lost and damned.

Proutt hated Westley; Proutt had in his hands Reck, a dog well-beloved by Westley. And Reck was pliant in Proutt's hands, both because Proutt knew dogs and because Reck was by nature tractable, eager to please, anxious to do that which he was asked to do. The combination presented itself to Proutt full clearly, as he walked his homeward way that day, and it is to be supposed that he fought out what fight there was within himself, during that long walk, and through the evening that followed.

That Proutt had some battle with himself cannot be denied. No man sets out to destroy a soul without first overcoming the scruples which bind him; and there were scruples in Proutt. There must have been. He loved dogs, loved fine dogs, and Reck was fine. Yet the destruction of Reck's honor and reputation and life—these were the ends which Proutt set himself to bring about, at what pain to his own heart no man may fully guess. It can only be known that in the end his hatred overweighed all else —that he threw himself into the thing he meant to do.

Reck, as has been shown, needed no training for his appointed work. Yet Proutt kept him, labored with him daily, for close to four long weeks, as all Fraternity men knew. None saw that training. It was known that Proutt took Reck far over the Sheepscot Ridge, where farms were all deserted; and no man was like to call upon him. But he had done that with dogs before, for woodcock lay thick in Sheepscot Valley. Once or twice men heard the barking of a dog in that valley; and there was a measure of pain in the notes. And three times men met Proutt driving homeward, with Reck lying weary and subdued upon the floor of the buggy, scarce fit to lift his head. It was remarked that Proutt was more dour and morose than ever; and Lee Motley thought the man was aging. . . .

One man only, and that man Jim Saladine, caught some inkling of that which was afoot. Jim was a deer hunter; and toward mid-October, with a shotgun under his arm for luck's sake, but never a buckshot in his cartridge pocket, he went one day into the Sheepscot Valley to search out the land. Deer lay in the swamps there; and Jim sought to locate them against the coming season. He moved slowly and quietly, as his custom was, ears and eyes open. And he saw many things which another man would never have seen.

Two things he saw which had significance. Once, in a muddy patch along the Sheepscot's brim, he came upon a deer's track; and other tracks beside it. A man's track, and a dog's.

Jim studied these tracks. They were sadly muddled and he could make little of them. But he was sure of this much—that man and dog had been attentive to the tracks of the deer. And this stayed in Jim's mind, because no dog in Fraternity has any business with the track of a deer, and no man may justly set a dog upon such track.

Later that day Jim was to find some explanation for what he had seen. Where Fuller's brook comes into the Sheepscot there lies an open meadow half a mile long, and half as broad; and near the lower end of the meadow half a dozen alders group about a lone tree in the open. Deer and moose, coming up the Sheepscot Valley, are like to cross the stream below and then traverse this meadow; and Jim Saladine stopped under cover at the meadow's head—it was near dusk—to see what he should see.

He saw what you may see any day along the Sheep-scot, and what, by the same token, you may go a weary year without seeing. He saw a deer, a proud buck, come up from the stream and follow the meadow toward where he lay. It passed the isolated alder clump, and some-thing there gave it alarm, for Jim saw its head lift—saw then the quick leap and rush which carried the creature to cover and away. . . .

Saw something else. Out from the alder clump burst a man, driving before him a dog. Dusk was falling. Jim saw their figures only dimly. But this much he saw. The man urged the dog after the deer with waving arms; and the dog, ever looking backward shamefacedly, trotted slowly off upon the trail, the man still urging from behind.

They slipped into the brush where the deer had gone, and Jim caught no further glimpse of them.

Now, Saladine was an honest man, who loved the deer he hunted; and he was angry. But he was also a just man; and he could not be sure whom he had seen. So it was that he kept a still tongue, and waited, and through the weeks that followed he watched, patiently enough, for what should come.

He meant, in that hour, to take a hand.

With a week of October left, Proutt took Reck home to Westley. Westley was not there, but Mrs. Westley marked Proutt's lowering eye, and was frightened of the man, and told Westley so when he came. But Westley was well enough pleased to have Reck back again, and he bade her forget Proutt.

Proutt had been, thus far, somewhat favored by fortune. The business of his office had taken Westley away from Fraternity for two weeks at a time, so that Proutt had had full time to do with Reck as he chose. Fraternity knew nothing of what had happened, though Jim Saladine may have guessed. There was one night at Will's store when Jim and Proutt were near fisticuffs. Proutt had brought Dan with him to the store; and Jim, studying the surly dog, asked:

"Dan ever notice a deer, Proutt?"

Proutt exclaimed profanely. "No," he said.

"I was over in the Sheepscot the other day," said Jim evenly. "See tracks where a dog had been after a deer."

"More like it was one of these setters," Proutt declared, watching them all from beneath lowered lids. "They'll kill a deer, or a sheep, give 'em a chance."

"It was hound's tracks," Jim persisted mildly; and something in Jim's tone, or in Proutt's own heart, made the trainer boil into fury, so that he strode toward Saladine. But Will Bissell came between, and the matter passed.

Proutt, before this, had taken Reck home; and the Westleys made much of the dog. Reck had affable and endearing little tricks of his own. He had a way of giving welcome, drawing back his upper lip so that his teeth showed as though in a snarl, yet panting with dog laughter all the time; and he had a way of talking, with high whines of delight, or throaty growls that ran the scale. And he would lie beside Westley, or beside Westley's wife, and paw at them until they held his paw in their hands, when he would go contentedly enough to sleep.

They thought the dog was unhappy when he came home to them. He had a slinking, shamed way about him. At first Westley supposed Proutt had whipped him; but Reck showed no fear of a whip in Westley's hands. After two or three days this furtiveness passed away and Reck was the joyously affectionate creature he had always been. So the Westleys forgot his first attitude of guilt, and loved him ardently as men and women will love a dog.

Westley had opportunity for one day's hunting with him, and Reck never faltered at the task to which he had been born and bred.

He had one fault. Chained, he would bark at the least alarm, in a manner to wake the neighborhood. So Westley had never kept him chained. It was not the way of Fraternity to keep dogs in the house of nights; so Reck slept in the woodshed, and Westley knocked a plank loose and propped it, leaving Reck an easy avenue to go out or in. It was this custom of Westley's which gave Proutt the chance for which he had laid his plans.

October had gone; November had come. This was in the days when woodcock might be shot in November if you could find them. But most men who went into the woods bore rifles, for it was open season for deer. Now and then you might hear the snapping crash of a thirty-thirty in Whitcher Swamp, or at one of the crossings, or—if you went so far—in the alder vales along the Sheepscot. And one day in the middle of the month, when the ground was frozen hard, Proutt came to Nick Westley's home.

He came at noon, driving his old buggy. Westley was at dinner when he heard Proutt drive into the yard; and he went to the door and bade the dog trainer come in. But Proutt shook his head, and his eyes were somber.

"You come out, Westley," he said. "I've a word for you."

There was something in Proutt's tone which disturbed Westley. He put on his mackinaw, and drew his cap down about his ears, and went out into the yard. Reck had been asleep on the doorstep when Proutt appeared; he had barked a single bark. But now he was gone into the shed, out of sight; and when Westley came near Proutt's buggy, the dog trainer asked:

"Did you see Reck sneak away?"

Westley was angry; and he was also shaken by a sudden tremor of alarm. He said hotly enough, "Reck never sneaks. He did not sneak away."

"He knows I saw him," said Proutt. "He heard me yell."

Westley asked with narrowing eyes, "What are you talking about? Where did you see him?"

"This morning," Proutt declared. "Scant daylight. Down in the swamp."

Westley stood very still, trying to remember whether he had seen Reck early that morning. And he could only remember, with a shocking certainty, that Reck had not been at home when he came out of the house to do his chores. He had called and got no answer; and it may have been half an hour before the dog appeared. It had disturbed Westley at the time; and he scolded Reck for self-hunting. But any dog will range the home farm in the morning hours, and Westley had not taken the matter seriously.

Proutt's words, and his tone more than his words, made the matter very serious indeed. Westley forced himself to ask, "What were you doing in the Swamp?"

"I was after a deer," said Proutt; and when Westley remained silent, Proutt added huskily, "So was Reck."

Westley cried, "That's a lie." But his own voice sounded strange and unnatural in his ears. He would not believe. Yet he knew that other dogs had chased deer in the past, and would again. He had himself shot half a dozen. It was the law; and he was the instrument of the law. And this was the very bitterness of Proutt's accusation; for if it were true, then he must shoot Reck. And Westley would have as soon shot one of his own blood as the dog he loved.

In the little instance of silence that followed upon his word, he saw all this, too clearly. And in spite of his love for Reck, and in spite of his ardent longing to believe that Proutt had lied, he feared desperately that the man spoke truth. Westley's wife would never have believed, for a woman refuses to believe any evil of those she loves. She is loyal by refusing to believe; a man may believe and be loyal still.

Westley did not know whether to believe or not, but he knew that he was terribly afraid. He told Proutt: "That's a lie!" And Proutt, after a long moment, clucked to his horse and started on. Westley called after him: "Wait!"

Proutt stopped his horse; and Westley asked, "What are you going to do?"

"You're game warden," Proutt told him sullenly. "Nobody around here can make you act, unless you've a mind to. But I've told you what's going on."

Westley was sweating in the cold, and said pitifully, "Proutt, are you sure?"

"Yes," said Proutt, and Westley cried, "What did you see?"

"I had a deer marked," said Proutt slowly. "He'd been feeding under an old apple tree down there. I was there before day this morning, figuring to get a shot at him. Crept in quiet. Come day, I couldn't see him. But after a spell I heard a smashing in the brush, and he come out through an open, and was away before I could shoot. And hot after him came Reck."

"How far away?" Westley asked.

"No more'n ten rod."

"You couldn't be sure."

"Damn it, man. I know Reck. Besides, I wouldn't want to say it was him, would I? He's a grand dog."

"What did you do?" Westley asked.

"Yelled at him to come in."

"Did he stop?"

"Stopped for one look, and then one jump into the brush and away he went."

Westley was almost convinced; he turned to call Reck, with some curious and half-formed notion that he might catechize the dog himself. But when he turned, he found Reck at his side; and the setter was standing steadily, legs stiff and proud like a dog on show, eyes fixed on Proutt. There was no guilt in his attitude; nor was there accusation. There was only steady pride and self-respect; and Westley, at sight of him, could not believe this damning thing.

He said slowly, "Look at him, Proutt. If this were true,

he'd be ashamed, and crawling. You saw some other dog."

Proutt shook his head. "He's a wise, bold dog, is Reck. Wise as you and me. He'll face it out if he can."

Westley pulled himself together, dropping one hand on Reck's head. "I don't believe it, Proutt," he said. "But I'm going to make sure."

"I am sure," said Proutt. "You can do as you please. But don't ask me to keep my mouth shut. You was quick enough to shoot Jackson's dog when you caught her on that doe."

"I know," said Westley and his face was white. "I'll be as quick with Reck, when I'm sure."

"You'll take pains not to get sure."

Westley held his voice steady. "Did you ever have to call Reck off of deer tracks?"

"No."

"Then he's never been taught not to run them?"

"Neither had Jackson's dog."

"What I mean," said Westley, "is this. He doesn't know it's wrong to run deer."

"That's no excuse."

"I'm not excusing him."

Proutt swore. "Well, what are you doing?"

"I'm going to take him into the swamp and find a deer," said Westley slowly. "See what he does. He's never been taught not to run them. So he'll run any that we find. If it's in him to do it, he'll take after them—"

Proutt nodded; and there was a certain triumph in his eyes. "You take your gun along," he said. "You're going to need that gun."

Westley, white and steady, said, "I'll take the gun. Will you come along?"

"Sure."

"Do you know where we can find a deer?"

"No; not this time of day."

Westley turned toward the house. "Wait," he said. "I'll get my gun; and we'll go pick up Jim Saladine. He'll know."

Proutt nodded. "I'll wait," he agreed.

Westley went into the house. Reck stood on the doorstep. Proutt, waiting, watched Reck with a flickering deadly light in his sullen eyes.

Saladine listened silently to Westley's request; but he looked at Proutt with an eye before which Proutt uneasily turned away his head. Nevertheless, being by nature a taciturn man, he made no comment or suggestion. He only said, "I can find a deer."

"Where?" Westley asked.

"Over in the Sheepscot," said Saladine. "I've got mine for this season, but I know some hardwood ridges over there where they're like to be feeding, come evening."

Proutt said uneasily, "Hell, there's a deer nearer than Sheepscot."

"Where?" asked Saladine.

"Everywhere."

"We ain't got time to cover that much territory today," the hunter said mildly. "If the Sheepscot suits, I'll go along. I'm most sure we'll pick up deer."

Westley asked, "Do you think I'm testing Reck fair?"

Saladine spat. "Yes, I'd say so," he agreed.

"I've got work to do," Proutt still objected. "Sheepscot's a danged long way."

"I want you to come," said Westley.

So Proutt assented at last; and they set off in his team. He and Westley in the front seat, Saladine and Reck behind. A five-mile drive over the Sheepscot Ridge. "Past Mac's Corner," Saladine told them, and they went that way.

The road took them by Proutt's house; and old Dan, Proutt's hound, came out to bark at them, and saw Proutt, and tried to get into the buggy. Proutt bade him back to the house; then, as an afterthought, got out and shut the hound indoors. "Don't want him following," he said.

Saladine's eyes were narrow with thought, but he made no comment, and they moved on their way.

That part of Maine in which Fraternity lies is a curious study for geologists. A good many centuries ago, when the great glaciers graved this land, they slid down from north to south into the sea, and in their sliding plowed deep furrows, so that the country is cut up by ridges, running almost true north and south, and ending in peninsulas with bays between. Thus the coast line is jagged as a saw.

These ridges run far up into the state; and the Sheepscot Ridge is as bold as any one of them. There is no break in it; and it herds the little waterways down into Sheepscot River, and guides the river itself south till it meets the sea. There are trout in Sheepscot; and thirty years ago the valley was full of farms and mills; but these farms are for the most part deserted now, and the mills are gone, leaving only shattered dams to mark the spots where they stood. The valley is a tangle of second-growth timber, broken here and there by ancient meadows through which brooks meander. Here dwells every wild thing that the region knows.

Proutt's old buggy climbed the long road up the eastern slope of the ridge; and the somber beauty of the countryside lay outspread behind them. The sun was falling lower; the shadows were lengthening; and a cold wind blew across the land. Across George's Valley and George's Lake lay the lower hills, the Appleton Ridge beyond, and far southeast the higher domes of Megunticook and the Camden Hills. The bay itself could not be seen, but the dark top of Blue Hill showed, twenty miles beyond the bay; and Mount Desert, ten miles farther still. . . .

The men had no eyes for these beauties. They rode in silence, watching the road ahead. And they passed through Liberty, and past Mac's Corner, and so up to top the ridge at last. Paused there to breathe Proutt's horse.

Back at Proutt's home, about the time they were in Liberty, someone had opened the door of the shed in which old Dan was locked; and the hound, watching his chance, scuttled out into the open. What well-founded habit prompted him can only be guessed; certain it is that he wheeled, never heeding the calls from behind him, and took the road by which Proutt had gone, hard on his master's trail.

If the dog trainer had known this, matters might have turned out differently, but Proutt could not know.

The road from Sheepscot Ridge down into Sheepscot Valley is for the most part rough and little used. An occasional farmer comes this way; an occasional fisherman drops from the steep descent to the bridge. But the frost has thrown boulders up across the road; and grass grows between the ruts, and the young hardwood crowds close on either side. Down this road, at Saladine's direction, Proutt turned; and the westering sun shone through the leafless branches and laid a bright mosaic before the feet of the horse.

Halfway down the hill Saladine spoke. "Let's light out," he said. "We'll find something up along this slope."

Westley nodded; and Proutt, after a moment's hesitation, stopped his horse. They got out, and Reck danced about their feet. Proutt tied the horse to a sapling beside the road, and they climbed the ruined stone wall and turned into the wood. Westley alone had a gun; the others were unarmed.

The course Saladine set for them was straight along the slope, moving neither up nor down; and the three men, accustomed to the woods, went quickly. Westley spoke to Reck now and then. His only word was the hunter's command. "Get in there," he said. "Get in. Go on." And Reck ranged forward, and up, and down, covering a front of half a dozen rods as they advanced. Westley was in the middle, Saladine was below, Proutt above the other two.

Westley had suggested putting his hunting bell on Reck; but Proutt negatived that with a caustic word. "He'd know, then, you wanted birds," he said. "And, anyways, it'd scare the deer." So they followed the dog by sight or by the stirring of his feet among the leaves; and at times he was well ahead of them, and at times when he moved more slowly they were close upon his heels. At such moments Westley held them back till Reck should work ahead.

Whether Reck had any knowledge of what was in their minds, no man can say. There were moments when they saw he was uncertain, when he turned to look inquiringly back at them. But for the most part he worked steadily back and forth as a good dog will, quartering the ground by inches. And always he progressed along the ridge, and always they followed him. And Saladine, down the slope, watched Proutt as they moved on.

No man spoke, save that Westley urged Reck softly on when the dog turned back to look at them. And at the last, when they saw that Reck had found game, it needed no word to bring the three together, two or three rods behind the dog.

Reck, as the gunners say, was "marking game." Nose down, he moved forward, foot by foot; and now and then he stopped for long seconds motionless, as though at point, but always he moved forward again. And Westley felt the cold sweat upon his forehead; and he looked at Proutt and saw the dog trainer licking his tight lips. Only Saladine kept a steady eye upon the dog and searched the thickets ahead.

After a rod or two Reck stopped, and this time he did not move. And Westley whispered to the others, "Walk it up, whatever it is. Move in." So the men went slowly forward, eyes aching with the strain of staring into the shadows of the wood.

When Reck took his point he was well ahead of them. He held it while they came up beside him; and then, as they passed where the dog stood, something plunged in the brush ahead, and they all saw the swift flash of brown and the bobbing white tail as a buck deer drove straight away from them along the slope. And Proutt cried triumphantly:

"A deer! I said it. I told you so. Shoot, Westley. Shoot!"

Westley stood still as still, and his heart was sunk a hundred fathoms deep. His hand was shaking and his eyes were blurred with tears. For Reck, who had no rightful concern with anything that roved the woods save the creatures that go on the wing, had marked a deer. Enough to damn him! Had hunted deer!

He tried to lift the gun, but Saladine spoke sharply. "Hold on. Look at the dog. He didn't chase the deer."

Westley realized then that Reck was, in fact, still marking game, moving slowly on ahead of them. But Proutt cried, "He'd smelled it; he didn't see it go. Or there's another ahead."

"He didn't chase the deer," said Saladine. Westley, without speaking, moved forward behind the dog. And of a sudden his heart could beat again.

For they came to where the buck had been lying, to his bed, still warm. And Reck passed over this warm bed, where the deer scent was so strong the men could almost catch it themselves; passed over this scent as though it did not exist, and swung, beyond, to the right, and up the slope. The buck had gone forward and down.

"He's not after deer," said Saladine.

They knew what he was after in the next instant, for wings drummed ahead of them, and four partridges got up, huge, fleeting shadows in the darkening woods. And Reck's nose followed them in flight till they were gone, then swung back to Westley, wrinkling curiously, as though he asked:

"Why did you not shoot?"

Westley went down on his knees and put his arms about the dog's neck; and then he came to his feet uncertainly as Proutt exclaimed, "He was after deer. He knew we were watching. Took the birds."

Westley tried to find a word, but Saladine, that silent man, stepped forward.

"Westley," he said, "wait a minute. You, Proutt, be still."

They looked at him uncertainly, Proutt growling. And Saladine spat on the ground as though he tasted the unclean. "I've kept my mouth shut. Wanted to see. Meant to tell it in the end. Westley, Proutt broke your dog."

Westley nodded. "Yes." He looked at Proutt.

"He broke him to run deer."

Westley began to tremble, and he could not take his eyes from Saladine; and Proutt broke out in a roaring oath, till Saladine turned slowly upon him.

The deer hunter went on: "I waited to see. I knew what would come; but I wanted to see. A bird dog's bred to birds. If he's bred right, it's in him. Reck's bred right. You can make him run deer. Proutt did. But you can't make him like it. Birds are his meat. You saw that just now. He didn't pay any heed to that buck, but he did pay heed to the partridge."

Proutt cried, "Saladine, you can't say a thing like that!"

Saladine cut in. "I saw you. Month ago. Down by Fuller's Brook. A deer crossed there, up into the meadow. You was in the alders with Reck, and you tried to set him on. He wouldn't run, and you drove him. I saw you, Proutt."

Westley looked down at Reck; and he looked at Proutt, the trainer; and he looked back at Reck again. There was something in Reck's eyes which made him hot and angry; there was a pleading something in Reck's slowly wagging tail. . . . And Westley turned to Proutt, cool enough now, and he said:

"I can see it now, Proutt. I've known there was something, felt there was something." He laughed joyously. "Why, Proutt, you man who knows dogs. Didn't you know you could not kill the soul and the honor of a dog like mine? Reck is a thoroughbred. He knows his work. And you—"

He moved a little toward the other. "Proutt," he said, "I'm going to lick you till you can't stand."

Proutt's big head lowered between his shoulders. "So—" he said.

And Westley stepped toward him.

Saladine said nothing; Reck did not stir; and the woods about them were as still as still. It was in this silence, before a blow could be struck, that they heard the pound of running feet in the timber above them, and Saladine said swiftly: "Deer!"

He moved, with the word, half a dozen paces back by the way they had come, to an old woods road they had crossed and stood there, looking up the slope. Westley and Proutt forgot each other and followed him; and Reck stayed close at Westley's heel. They could hear the beating feet more plainly now, and Saladine muttered:

"Scared. Something chasing it."

On the word, abruptly startling them, the deer came into view—a doe, running swiftly and unwearied. Striking the woods road, the creature followed the easier going, down the slope toward them; and because they were so still it failed to discover the men till it was scarce two rods away. Sighting them then, the doe stopped an instant, then lightly leaped into the brush at one side, and was gone.

The men did not look after the deer; they waited to see what pursued it. And after a moment Saladine's face grimly hardened, and Westley's became somber and grave, and Proutt turned pale as ashes.

For, lumbering down the hill upon the deer's hot trail, came Dan, that hound which Proutt had shut away at home—came Dan, hot on the trail as Proutt had taught him.

The dog saw them, as the deer had done, and would have swung aside, but Proutt cried, in a broken voice: "Dan, come in."

So came the hound to heel, sullenly and slowly, eyes off into the wood where the doe had gone; and for a moment no one spoke, till Saladine slowly drawled:

"Westley, give Proutt your gun."

Westley did not speak. He was immensely sorry for Proutt, and all his anger at the man had gone. Proutt looked old, and shaken, and weary, and he had dropped his heavy hand across Dan's neck. He caught Westley's eye and said harshly, "To hell with your gun. I'll use my own."

An instant more they stood, then Westley turned to Saladine. "Jim, let's go," he said. And Saladine nodded, and they moved away, Reck at Westley's heels. After a moment, an odd panic in his voice, Proutt called after them: "Wait, I'll ride you home."

But Saladine answered: "I'll walk!" And Westley did

not speak at all. He and Reck and the deer hunter went steadily upon their way.

The sun was setting, and dark shadows filtered through the trees to hide old Proutt where he still stood beside his dog.